Alvin peered at Cupid Delaney over the rims of his glasses. "No one can see you or hear you? I almost feel sorry for you, poor kid. You don't know when to end a joke."

Cupid Delaney's sunny disposition was slowly turning cloudy. "It's no joke, I can assure you." She smiled coolly. "I really am an invisible cupid. And I have the powers to prove it."

Alvin rolled his eyes. "Oh, sure. Now we're talking powers. OK. How?"

"Meet me at the football field after school. Right after school, understand?"

He grinned. "You've got guts, I've got to admit. All right, I'll meet you. But if you're planning on inviting the Tooth Fairy or Tinker Bell or any of your other magical friends, count me out. I can only cope with you."

"Ha, ha." Cupid Delaney watched Alvin hurry down the hall. This is going to be harder than I envisioned, she thought. Yet deep down, she realized she was excited. That ugly/attractive boy had one of the strongest wills she had ever encountered, and to lock horns (and hearts) with him was going to prove a tough challenge—and maybe fun?

Hmmmm, she thought, I wonder if the Tooth Fairy is free this afternoon.

Ellen Leroe

Have a Heart, Cupid Delaney

BANTAM BOOKS
TORONTO · NEW YORK · LONDON · SYDNEY · AUCKLAND

RL 5, IL age 12 and up

No character in this book is intended to represent any actual person; all the incidents of the story are entirely fictional in nature.

This low-priced Bantam Book has been completely reset in a typeface designed for easy reading, and was printed from new plates. It contains the complete text of the original hardcover edition.
NOT ONE WORD HAS BEEN OMITTED.

HAVE A HEART, CUPID DELANEY

A Bantam Book / published by arrangement with E. P. Dutton

PRINTING HISTORY
E. P. Dutton edition published October 1986

Bantam edition / February 1988

ISBN 0-553-27002-8

Published simultaneously in the United States and Canada

Bantam Books are published by Bantam Books, a division of Bantam Doubleday Dell Publishing Group, Inc. Its trademark, consisting of the words "Bantam Books" and the portrayal of a rooster, is Registered in U.S. Patent and Trademark Office and in other countries. Marca Registrada. Bantam Books, 666 Fifth Avenue, New York, New York 10103.

PRINTED IN THE UNITED STATES OF AMERICA

KR   0 9 8 7 6 5 4 3 2

for Joy R. Weiner:
three-quarters special friend,
one-quarter cupid

Have a Heart,
Cupid Delaney

Cupid's Last Chance
at Romance

It was a flash of insight, a split second of what the Rosicrucian magazine ads called cosmic consciousness. The most rotten zap of consciousness she had ever experienced. One instant, as she finished signing her millionth valentine card, she was humming "All You Need Is Love," her head filled with thoughts of the "flying up" ceremony next month and getting her wings. Then, in the next instant, she had heard her name being called in the chocolate-coated sandpaper tone she dreaded, and knew so well. And she realized, in a terrible, plummeting second, that it was all over for her; she had messed up yet again. Her future would not include the certified cupid wings she had always dreamed of owning. Her happy days in the Love Bureau were over.

"Cupid Delaney!" The honey-drenched rasp came again, and before she had time to adjust her white shift or push back her tousled blonde curls, the imposing figure of the Sweetheart Squad leader, Valentina Amour, strode into view. As Cupid nervously stood up, her knee caught the edge of the table. It rocked perilously, the million valentines shifting from their precisely arranged piles. Cupid Delaney gasped "Oh, no!" and tried to right the table, but the endless pieces of paper flew in the air like brightly colored confetti and landed on the red-tiled floor. She fell to her knees, babbling apologies.

"All right, all right, just leave them for now," the statuesque woman cut her off, motioning for Cupid Delaney to get back to her feet. "Passionata can help you clean up the mess in a few minutes. Now, I want to talk to you."

A sermon from Valentina. The other cupids-in-training in the mail room eyed one another knowingly and then hurriedly left. On the Muzak system, Engelbert Humperdinck was crooning "Release Me." Cupid Delaney sighed. So this was how it was going to end. Two years of intense cupid training in the biggest, best-run Love Bureau in the Northeast with a direct line to the Great Goddess Herself. All to be shot down in an avalanche of valentines. And all because of what? Failing her Language of Love course? Mismatching those two romantically inclined teenagers last month in Painted Post, New York? How was she to know that Terry and Pat were both *male* names? It hadn't indicated that on the computer printouts. All right, so emergency romantic surgery was necessary to remedy the situation, but that wasn't enough to drop her from the training program, was it?

One quick look at Valentina's stern features and Cupid Delaney had her answer. How could someone so gorgeous, so goddesslike herself, have a heart of ice? Biting her lower lip, the young girl put her hands behind her back and began fiddling with the feathers of her arrows, a sure sign of frayed nerves. The Sweetheart Squad leader motioned her to a seat and pulled out a small, heart-shaped notebook from the folds of her diaphanous tunic. Murmuring

2

under her breath, she riffled through the pages and then stopped toward the back.

"Ah," Valentina said, "Woodside." She looked up and gazed directly into Cupid Delaney's puzzled eyes. "The site of your next assignment."

"My next—assignment?" Hope flared up. Or was this some cruel joke the Sweetheart leader was playing? But Valentina was a no-nonsense, efficient administrator.

"That's correct. An assignment. But if you bungle this one, well, I'm afraid it will be your last. You've already been put on probation twice this past month, and one more black mark will see you thrown out of the program."

Cupid Delaney winced but refrained from asking the inevitable question. She knew only too well what would happen to a failed cupid trainee. She had spotted too many of them below, trying their hands at writing cutesy, saccharine greeting-card lines or tutoring poetry appreciation to hostile or indifferent students. One or two less proud rejects worked at those awful singing telegram places where they were forced to wear phony cupid wings and tap dance in time to their musical message. Oh, it was too terrible to contemplate. Cupid Delaney shook her head and squared her shoulders. She was being given another chance. An assignment in some little town called Woodside. She gave her full attention to Valentina as the woman reeled off the pertinent facts of the case.

"You'll have two couples to work with, two teenage couples at Woodside High School in a suburban community called Woodside, New Jersey."

"New Jersey?"

Valentina's brows darkened. "What did you expect on a trial assignment, and a last one at that: Monaco? Paris?"

3

"Well, no, but New York City or San Francisco would have been nice. Well, no matter," she said hastily, "New Jersey is fine."

"I'm glad you think so." The squad leader's tone was cool, yet a glint of something—amusement?—flickered in her eyes. "If I may proceed? These two couples are hopelessly mismatched right now. We've got a special dance coming up on, let's see, Friday, a week from today. Their big homecoming dance, called, archaically enough, the Grid. Short for Gridiron, referring to football. It's very important to at least two of these four subjects to get asked to the event by the right person, and both of them are experiencing severe discomfort in the heart region. A sure sign our services are required. Agreed?"

Cupid Delaney nodded vigorously.

"Well, I'm glad to see we agree on something. All right, your assignment, Cupid Delaney, will be to pair the right couples together in time for this big homecoming dance. Now, let's go to the computer and get their printouts. You'll discover that— What's the matter now, for Venus' sake! You look stricken."

"Well, a week. I mean, that's only seven days away. That's not enough time to sort out this problem and get all the proper people in love with the right partners. Ever since the Instant Attraction Code was outlawed, it's been taking longer to initiate infatuation or even puppy love. I don't think I can do it. I can't."

Valentina drew herself up. Raising her face toward the heavens, she thumped the little notebook in time with her words, "Cupids"—*thump!*—"do not"—*thump! thump!*—"say can't"—big *thump!* "Romance is our trade"—*thump!*—"our skill"—*thump!*—"our goddess-given profession"—*thump!*

4

She jabbed a rosy-hued fingernail at Cupid Delaney's mesmerized face. "Do you want to fly up and earn your wings next month? Do you want to wear your heart on your sleeve and make us all proud at the Love Bureau?"

A nod, weak at first, and then strong.

"All right then, erase those negative words from your mind and follow me to the computer room."

She couldn't believe her luck. Cupid Delaney got up and trailed Valentina out the door and through the pink mists of the third floor to the computer chamber. The other cupid trainees giggled or averted their eyes when they spotted their less fortunate colleague in tow with the majestic leader. Cupid Delaney knew they were feeling relieved not to be in her shoes. Valentina Amour frightened all the cupids in the program; only the members of the Sweetheart Squad treated Valentina as an equal, and even then as a slightly special one.

The computer chamber was a droning, beeping, clattering assortment of noises and cheerful cherub types working the machines. Valentina swept into the room and immediately commandeered a unit.

"See, here." She jabbed crisply at the buttons and then stood back to allow Cupid Delaney to read the screen. "Your Woodside couples."

Cupid Delaney read off the four names and then did a double take.

"Oh, no," she murmured. "There must be a mistake."

Valentina frowned. "What are you talking about?"

"Well, uh, these four kids—"

"Subjects," Valentina interrupted. "We call them subjects or clients."

"Subjects, then," Cupid Delaney continued. "I entered this information a week ago and thought at the time how well suited the kids, er, subjects, were in their own natural romantic pairing. I mean, we've got the school quarterback, Craig Lacrosse, interested in the popular cheerleader, Dawn Cummings—"

"The hunks, or hunk and hunkette of Woodside," Valentina offered, obviously trying to make a joke and appear with-it.

Cupid Delaney winced and continued, "—And then we've got the rather eccentric brain, Alvin Danziger, who really likes the quiet loner, Helen Mapes."

"The nerd and nerdette." Valentina arched an eyebrow and waited for a responding giggle, but Cupid Delaney could only manage a weak, lopsided grin.

"Well, Squad Leader Amour," she said, feeling disaster raise its gigantic fist to smash her into tiny pieces, "the hunk and hunkette, as you put it, Craig and Dawn, seem perfectly suited and content with each other. And the nerd and nerdette, Alvin and Helen, appear likewise."

Lightning did not strike. The skies did not darken and threaten to suck her into a black hole. Valentina merely shook her head slowly, almost sadly, as if at a toddler who reached for a candy bar rather than a piece of fruit. "You just don't know, do you? What does romance mean to you? Does romance mean boring, predictable pairings, like Helen Mapes and Alvin Danziger, or great, combustive chemical reactions in which a hunk like Craig Lacrosse goes suddenly crazy about shy, withdrawn Helen? Or perhaps the most dazzling girl at school, the unattainable Dawn, falls for a loser like this Alvin character. That, my dear Cupid, is what love is all about. It's what causes the rose to bloom, puts the rainbows in the sky, makes the world go round." (Here we go again, thought Cupid Delaney, biting hard on the inside of her cheek to keep from laughing. Trot out all the old clichés about moon and June.) "Love is the miraculous, the unexpected, the great wish fulfillment of all time. I guarantee your so-called well-suited little nerds will fall all over themselves to walk into the big homecoming dance next Friday night on the arms of the most popular, beautiful people at school, Alvin with Dawn and quiet Helen with beauteous maximus Craig."

You want to make a bet? Cupid Delaney thought. She refused to buy the equation of Devastating Looks plus Personality times Unavailability equals Impassioned Attraction, and especially not with these four teenagers. There was a feeling she got when she studied their printouts, a sinking one. Somehow she knew there'd be trouble with this case. Maybe when she went down to Woodside this weekend to scout out her subjects and delve into their heads, she'd discover the secret yearnings that Valentina pronounced were there. She hoped so. If not, the assignment was going to be one of the most tricky to handle—yet she had to do it successfully. She had to pair the hunk with Ms. Nonentity and the beautiful cheerleader with Alvin. And not only pair them, but instill romantic fires into their hearts. Craig Lacrosse, King of the Heartbreakers, had to sleep, live, and breathe little Helen's name, had to lose his cool and self-control over this girl. And Dawn Cummings, a knockout and homecoming queen material, had to renounce her retinue of good-looking guys to zero in on the school eccentric, Alvin Danziger.

Cupid Delaney sighed. She knew in her soul it wasn't going to be easy. She made one last attempt to dissuade the squad leader from sending her on this mission, but Valentina was not to be moved. She stood in front of the computer, arms tightly crossed, a set line to those movie-star lips. At the end she merely shook her head.

"I'm giving you one of the easiest assignments to hit the Love Bureau in ages. Alvin and Helen will succumb all too readily—and happily—to Dawn's and Craig's charms."

"But in a week? Can't I get an extension?"

Valentina patted her glossy black hair, then fixed piercing green eyes on Cupid Delaney. "One week," she intoned. "Seven days. That's when the dance is and that's when the transformation has to take place. Trust me, this will be a snap. Now, are there any further questions?"

Yes, Cupid Delaney wanted to say. What's the address of the nearest singing telegram office?

The Hunk

Saturday evening, Date Night U.S.A.

Craig Lacrosse seemed to take it very seriously.
The handsome Woodside senior had spent over an
hour showering, blow-drying his thick golden
brown hair, selecting an appropriate cologne, and
then scrutinizing the depths of his bedroom closet.
He now appeared to have the perfect outfit in mind
and began to untie the belt of his short terry
bathrobe. Over on the dresser, hidden behind a
football trophy, Cupid Delaney tried to squeeze her
eyes shut in sudden embarrassment. Then she
remembered. Butterflies don't have eyelids.

She was reprieved. Craig kept his robe on,
yanked out a shirt, and then looked down at it with a
frown. Muttering, he padded over to his door and
shouted "Beth!", then went to the dresser and flung
the shirt on top. From beside the base of the trophy,
two inches from the material, Cupid Delaney
folded in her wings and trembled. For goodness'
sake, why couldn't the Love Bureau assign different
disguises to their agents? Why did they always have
to be butterflies?

"Because they're delicate creatures of nature
that can travel easily on assignment," Valentina

Amour had answered at a morning meeting. "What would you suggest instead, Cupid Delaney, a leopard or gorilla suit?" Everyone had giggled, but Cupid Delaney was thinking more along the lines of ladybugs. They were small, delicate creatures of nature, too, but they were tinier, less apt to be noticed, could make faster escapes. She wanted to write up her suggestion and put it in the *Love Bureau Bulletin,* the interconstellation newspaper, but she sensed Valentina's disapproval and kept silent. Why was everyone so irked by her way of thinking? Didn't they encourage cupids to be freethinkers? Apparently not. Why else had she gotten into all the scrapes these last few months, if not for her determination to do things her way? And her way was not the way of the Love Bureau.

But if she failed this Woodside case, she'd be thrown out of the program, and she couldn't imagine a life without wings and romantic purpose. So, she told herself, pay attention. Keep still. Glean all you can from this vain first subject. And most important of all, *don't get caught!* At least this time she had been given the small New Guinea golden variety of butterfly, rather than the larger, more colorful swallowtail. Granted, her wings were a striking medley of yellow, black, and orange, but folded up as tiny as she could be, as she was now behind the trophy, she was nearly invisible.

Or so she thought until Beth (Craig's mother?) entered the disorganized bedroom and cried, "What in the world is that?" And pointed directly at her. But no, she was pointing to the arm of the shirt, draped an inch from Cupid's hiding place.

Craig screwed up his handsome face. "A very wrinkled shirt. The one I want to wear tonight for my date with Tiffany."

Mrs. Lacrosse, a pretty blonde with her son's even features, raised her eyebrows. "You can't go out in a mess like that." (Here, Cupid Delaney felt like saying, you iron it.) "Here," Mrs. Lacrosse continued, picking up the shirt, "let *me* iron it. I know you want to look perfect tonight."

As if he doesn't come close right now, Cupid Delaney thought, peering at the boy objectively. Truly, you could say all you liked about Adonis or Hercules; they were OK guys as far as gods go, but Craig Lacrosse had something, an oomph, a *je ne sais quoi,* that really made him stand out. He was tall and lean, yet surprisingly muscular. Crowned with thick golden brown hair that framed paperback-romance-novel features and incredible crystal blue eyes, he made your heart beat faster with his sexy grin.

Was Craig Lacrosse enchanting because adoring fans looked at him and wanted to believe he had everything? Cupid Delaney wondered. Was it just in their wishful imaginations and, like the emperor with no clothes, was he fooling everyone? She had to know. She had to find out all about this boy before she went to work. How else could she determine the right way to penetrate his defenses and make him lose his heart to Helen Mapes? That is, *if* he had a heart. Right now she wasn't so sure. The King of the Heartbreakers could be heartless himself.

Certainly he was lazy and manipulative. He called his mother Beth; she treated him like a helpless baby, rushing up the stairs at his command, pleading to iron his shirt. What next? Cupid Delaney thought. She didn't have to wait long.

"When you're done with the shirt," Craig was saying, digging around the dresser, fingers nearly touching a butterfly wing, "would you call Cynthia Walker for me? Here, take my address book." He proffered what looked like the Los Angeles telephone directory to his mother's eagerly outstretched hands. "Tell her I had late practice tonight but I'll pick her up at nine thirty, in time to catch the last show at the Rialto."

"But I thought you said you were seeing Tiffany?"

Craig chuckled, then winked. "I am. But Tiffany's only round one of the evening. She's invited me to dinner tonight at her house—"

"Oh, Craig, baby, the Huntington-Hatherford estate?"

He nodded, obviously pleased with himself. "How could I refuse? But I promised Cynthia to take her to this movie for her birthday, so I'll have to cut out of the big family dinner before dessert. I don't have time, but if you could call up Cynthia and make the excuse for me, I'd really appreciate it."

Mrs. Lacrosse cooed at him, delighted to be performing some service, any service, dishonest or not, for the beloved Sun God.

"Beth!" an irritated voice boomed up the stairs. "What's taking so long up there? The Goldmans should be arriving any minute."

"Your father," Mrs. Lacrosse sighed, winking conspiratorially. She leaned out the door. "I'm working on Craig's love life. I'll be down in a second."

From down below came a proud laugh. "A second? Try a year. With the love life our son's got, it could take even longer. A real love-'em-and-leave-'em type."

The doorbell rang and Mrs. Lacrosse made a face. "The Goldmans, right on time as usual. I better go and greet them, otherwise your father will have a fit."

"But what about the shirt?" demanded her son in a petulant tone.

"Don't you worry." Mrs. Lacrosse patted the item as if it were a newborn baby. "I'll have it ironed perfectly in less than ten minutes."

"I knew you'd come through. Thanks, Beth."

Cupid Delaney felt like making a rude noise, but a butterfly raspberry was inaudible. She settled for wrinkling her bug eyes in disgust. This was too much. Craig was too much. Everything about him was larger than life—his looks, his charm, his string of girlfriends—yet somehow not real. If she wanted to succeed in the assignment, and she wanted to more than anything in the world, she had to find the one flaw, the one insecurity, the one quality that made the popular quarterback vulnerable and therefore open to attack and transformation. But what could it be? What?

And then the impossible happened. For once luck fell her way. Craig said the words that gave her ammunition, or at least the potential for invading his emotional fortress.

"Oh, by the way, Dawn hasn't called, has she?" It was said offhandedly, but Cupid Delaney's precise romantic radar could pick up the tension in the air.

"Who, dear?"

"Dawn. Dawn Cummings. The captain of the varsity cheerleaders. She stopped by the house with some friends the day you had your bridge party."

Mrs. Lacrosse puckered her forehead in thought, and as she deliberated, Craig made an impatient sound.

"Baby, I don't think so," his mother said, "but I could check with Wanda or your father. Why, is it important to you?"

"What, if Dawn called? Oh, no, not at all." Craig airily waved and gave a convincing laugh, but Cupid Delaney was not so easily convinced.

"She just mentioned at school yesterday that she wanted to talk to me about something important, and, well, I assumed she'd be calling me over the weekend, but . . ." His voice dwindled off and he jammed his hands in the pockets of his robe.

Mrs. Lacrosse eyed him in astonishment. "A girl says she wants to talk to you and she doesn't call back? Who does that to *you*? What did she want, a date?"

"I don't know, but it's nothing to get all frosted about, Beth, OK?"

But he was now pulling out socks from the lower drawer and jamming on a brown sock next to a black. Cupid Delaney hopped up and down in excitement. Obviously, it *was* something to get frosted about. The fact that a girl did not pursue him was irritating the boy and making him behave irrationally. Or was it more than that? Was it because it was Dawn Cummings?

Mrs. Lacrosse gently leaned down and handed her son the right color mate to his black sock. "She's either crazy or got cold feet. Or else she's playing the oldest game in the book and trying to make you jealous."

Spoken like a true mother. Cupid Delaney grinned. The thought that maybe an attractive girl would not be interested in her son or had simply forgotten to call was not to be given credibility. The hunk of Woodside High shot down by indifference? Unheard of!

And Craig now smiled and murmured, "Of course, she's doing it on purpose. Why else wouldn't she call?" He straightened up, a blond demigod in a cutoff terry bathrobe and two black-stockinged feet, and laughingly shooed his mother out the door.

Cupid Delaney edged slowly around the base of the trophy into the light and then darted back as Craig came to stand in front of the dresser. Fluffing his attractively disheveled hair, he stared into the mirror and grinned at the tall, sexy boy who had it all.

"Little Miss Cheerleader thinks she can fool me?" he said with a chuckle. "No way. I've got her number now. And I may just make her wait a little longer before I ask her to the Grid next week."

A tap on the door and a sandy-haired, older version of Craig poked his head in. "What's all this, talking to yourself these days?"

Craig laughed. "Yeah, Dad, it's all this Saturday-night pressure. I can't keep up."

Mr. Lacrosse shook his head proudly. "My son, the heartbreaker."

"Yeah." The heartbreaker grinned. "It's a dirty job and tough work, but someone's got to do it."

When his father laughed and then turned down the hall, Cupid Delaney seized her chance. She unfolded her wings and, sensing a draft, headed instinctively for the open bathroom window. She had learned one essential fact about Craig tonight. Somehow Dawn had gotten through his "love-'em-and-leave-'em" façade by playing it cool. He definitely was interested in the pretty cheerleader. Why else consider taking her to the homecoming dance? Yet if he was attracted to Dawn, why was he dating up such a storm with all these other girls? Safety in numbers? Afraid to get involved and possibly get hurt? Maybe that was Craig Lacrosse's secret fear, Cupid Delaney thought. He sure talked about being heartless, but what was that famous line: Methinks the *lady-killer* doth protest too much!

With inward glee, Cupid Delaney soared out the window into the cold November night. Might as well do both hunks at the same time and get her heavy socializing over with at one fell swoop. Next stop: Dawn Cummings's house.

The Hunkette

Dawn Cummings was not home.

The cheerleader was instead turning down dances at Streamers, Woodside's hot dance club and favorite hangout of the local college crowd. The no-alcohol restriction on Saturday night allowed the high school kids access to the club, with its dazzling ceiling mirrors and unusual wall decor, but Dawn wasn't impressed by the exotic surroundings. Or by the pulsing music blasting from the barely legal sound system. She was hot, tired, and slowly realizing that tonight had been a mistake.

When Tom Delacruz held out his hand to lead her to the tiny dance floor, she frowned and backed away, almost crushing a frightened butterfly, who had just landed at the foot of her table. Cupid Delaney yelped and then held her breath, certain the noise had penetrated the sounds of the crowd. But seconds later she realized a cannon suddenly exploding would have as much, or as little, impact as her shriek. No one could hear anything except the music. Tom, a darkly attractive senior and line-backer for the Woodside Pirates football team, raised his voice to make himself understood, but Dawn pretended she couldn't hear and returned to

17

the table. There she sank into her seat with a grateful sigh and wiggled out of her tight heels. Seizing her chance, the little butterfly slowly inched her way up the leg of Dawn's designer jeans and then quickly landed, almost upside down, beneath the rim of the table.

Something soft and warm and sticky sweet seemed to be her landing pad. Puzzled, Cupid Delaney tried to lift a leg. Nothing happened. She yanked harder. This time her tiny body sank, as if into deadly quicksand. And then it hit her. She had stumbled upon someone's used wad of bubble gum! Talk about gumming up the works, she thought, smiling weakly, and then burst into tears.

Up in the viewing room of the Love Bureau, Passionata suddenly saw a red light begin to blink in the New Jersey sector.

"Enchantée!" she cried. "Get Valentina in here. Fast! We have a cupid in trouble."

The Senior Sweetheart member hurried off, returning in seconds with an irate Valentina.

"What's so important to drag me away from 'The Love Boat'? You know it's my favorite—what? A cupid in trouble? Who is it? Quickly."

Red-haired and delicate-featured Passionata punched some buttons, and a picture of Streamers came into view.

"Fine-tune, fine-tune," Valentina snapped. "Find her."

The screen narrowed down to pick up a terrified-looking butterfly, helplessly entangled in a sticky wad of bubble gum.

"Honestly," Valentina said, shaking her thick, loose hair. "I should have guessed it was Delaney. I'm halfway tempted to leave her in that state."

"Oh, no," Enchantée said, "you wouldn't. Look at her. She's practically all cried out."

"Help her, Valentina," Passionata implored. "She can't help it that she's a little clumsy and tends to, well . . ."

"Bungle things? Honestly!" Valentina rolled her eyes. "All right, all right. For both your sakes, and because I'm such a gracious, loving creature" (Passionata and Enchantée exchanged secret, amused glances), "I'll extricate the girl from her dilemma. But she's on her own from now on."

Valentina stared at the screen intently for several seconds, then fingered a heart-shaped crystal hanging around her neck on a gossamer-thin chain. There was silence in the room; then a bolt of lightning crashed and down below—

The chewing gum tightened up, became as smooth as glass, and Cupid Delaney cried out as she fell from the trap. Like a cat, however, she managed to land safely, nothing broken, not even a dented wing.

"A miracle," she said. "I could have been stuck forever. Unless . . . ?" Casting wondering eyes upward, she whispered, "Thank you." She was grateful now that the Love Bureau monitored their cupids so closely. The way she should be monitoring her own subject right this very minute.

She took a deep breath and inched her way back to the battlefront, this time making certain her hiding place was clean and safe. The back of the table leg allowed her a full view of her subject, and right now her subject didn't look too happy. Cupid Delaney couldn't understand it. From what the printouts and research had revealed, Dawn Cummings was a natural flirt who loved to party, dance, and just generally play the field. And because she was so pretty and had the distinct advantage of being captain of the varsity cheerleaders as well as

19

head of the newly organized and very elite Spirit Club, or activities committee, at school, she had ample opportunity to mingle with and dazzle the many males she met. And yet tonight, Streamers, the ideal environment for a partygoer like Dawn, seemed to hold no interest for her. If anything, she was aloof and antisocial, refusing to dance and failing to respond to all the attention from her date, Tom, and the three other boys who surrounded her table.

When Dawn tossed back her glossy long hair with a frown and then leaned close to the girl sitting next to her, Cupid Delaney moved in also.

"I don't know about you, Wendy, but I can't take too much more of this. I've got to get out of here."

Wendy Chu, Dawn's closest female friend, a fellow varsity cheerleader, looked at her in astonishment. She began to sputter, but Dawn cut her off.

"Just follow my lead," she whispered. Then she gazed with limpid violet eyes at Tom, who had just returned to the table and was trying to locate a seat. "Don't sit down yet, Tom. Wendy's got a favor to ask you."

Wendy opened her mouth, but Dawn quickly continued. "She's embarrassed to tell you, but she has a splitting headache. Could you go ask the waiter if he can find an aspirin for her? And while you're up, could you bring us back some more diet colas? And water for Wendy?"

"Anything else?" Tom asked with a trace of sarcasm, but when Dawn awarded him a dazzling smile, he seemed to melt and left eagerly. Probably hoping to return three notches higher in Dawn's favor, Cupid Delaney thought, and couldn't blame him. If ever there was a modern-day version of the quintessential charmer, Scarlett O'Hara, Dawn

Cummings was it. All she needed was a big, floppy hat, a crinoline or two, and a mint julep in her hand. She could be cranky, aloof, or sarcastic; she could ignore the boys in her company and refuse to laugh at their jokes or to dance with them, but let the charm come out momentarily, like the sun on a cloudy day, and instantly all was forgiven.

What was it? Cupid Delaney wondered, peering intently at the girl. Was it, like Craig, the exceptional looks? And yet if you examined her face feature by feature, Dawn was not beautiful or even really pretty. The layered, thick hair cascading around her shoulders, the model's figure, the perfectly accessorized outfit, all these things contributed to her "look." But what really clinched it and made Dawn *appear* to be a 10 when actually she bordered on 6 was her attitude. She believed she was a 10. And so everyone else did, too. It was in her walk, her contrary behavior, her little games, and her eye contact. Here was a winner, you thought, whenever Dawn Cummings appeared. A girl who had it all. And naturally, you wanted to get close to a winner. You hoped the magic would rub off on you. And if it didn't, well, it had to be your fault, not hers.

So far Cupid Delaney had picked up nothing new from her surveillance. Dawn Cummings, the stereotypical popular cheerleader, attractive, moody, flirtatious, was just as she appeared on the surface and from the printouts. But there had to be more, as in Craig's case. A gorgeous senior of her caliber was not about to dive off the deep end for a quirky, eccentric junior named Alvin, for Zeus' sake! Unless she secretly pined for studious, ho-hum nerds with chipmunk names. Cupid Delaney doubted it very, very much. So how could she find the vulnerable spot that would enable her to manipulate Dawn's heart?

Before Cupid could take any time to ponder the question, Dawn had risen, pulling a startled Wendy up with her.

"Uh, excuse us," Dawn said brightly, "but we're just going to the little girls' room. Powder our noses and all that female stuff."

The little girls' room? Cupid Delaney winced. Powder our noses? How coy could you get? Only someone like Dawn could get away with lines like those. And Wendy was saying, "But I don't have to— Ouch! Oh, yes, I do." She rubbed the part of the foot that had been deliberately stepped on and now was babbling about fixing her hair and putting on fresh lipstick.

The good stuff, Cupid Delaney exulted. The nitty-gritty. Everyone knew what this social custom really signified: digging the dirt, spreading the gossip, getting the lowdown on feelings and secrets. All that other stuff, biological or cosmetic, was just an excuse to pull your best girlfriend into the "confessional."

She now realized her best chance for eavesdropping was going to slip out of her fingers, er, wings, unless she did something fast. Cupid Delaney watched Dawn pick up her small clutch and then Wendy bend down for her larger, open tote. Taking what felt like a kamikaze leap, Cupid Delaney closed her eyes and plunged into the murky depths of the girl's unzipped handbag. She scuttled inside a small makeup case and then slid over a log pile of eye-makeup pencils and lipstick tubes. It didn't matter how uncomfortable she was, however. The end result was what mattered, and hopefully, that was going to be the unbaring of Dawn Cummings' soul.

The roller coaster ride ended in the women's room. As soon as Wendy plunked the large tote down on the floor beneath the sink, Cupid Delaney felt safe enough to venture forth from the eyeliner pencils and climb to the top of the bag. If either girl had looked down, she would have gotten the shock of her life by observing two black, beady eyeballs peering up at her from behind the zipper. But neither girl was looking down. They were too engrossed in conversation. And what conversation! Cupid Delaney realized, rubbing her front feelers together in anticipation.

"What in the world is wrong with you tonight?" Wendy was saying, perching on the counter and staring at her friend. "You're behaving like a social zombie. Tom must think he asked out an extra from *Night of the Living Dead.*"

"Thank you very much," Dawn said. "You always did give the nicest compliments." She pulled a brush from her bag and began raking it through her long hair with quick, angry strokes.

Wendy hesitated, waited until the room was empty, and then said, "Dawn, what is it? It isn't like you to act this way."

"It isn't like me to be treated this way," Dawn retorted and then flung the brush down and faced her friend. "Wendy, I am having a perfectly miserable time, and I can't help showing it. I wanted so much for this date to work out between Tom and me, but it isn't. And I feel awful."

"Oh, don't you believe it. Tom's thrilled you agreed to go out with him. He told me on the way over to your house that he's going to ask you to the Grid."

"You don't understand!" Dawn wailed. "I don't want Tom to ask me to the Grid. I don't want to date him."

"But, but . . . you just said . . ." Wendy was confused, and her normally cheerful, smiling face clouded over.

"It's not Tom I want," Dawn said in an intense, low voice. "It's Craig Lacrosse." (Bingo! thought Cupid Delaney, almost falling back into the tote with excitement.) "I don't care at all about Tom Delacruz. He was supposed to be the person to make Craig jealous."

"You mean because he and Craig are so tight? On school council and the Pirates? You thought Tom would go back after this evening singing your praises to Craig, and then Craig would realize what he's missing and call you and ask you to the dance?"

Dawn nodded, her lower lip pouting even more noticeably. "I feel so miserable, Wendy! Everyone's assuming Craig and I will go together. Well, it's a sure thing that he's going to be elected homecoming king and I'll be elected—well, I mean, I *may* be chosen one of the princesses."

Wendy hooted. "Don't play modest with me, Cummings. You were going to say 'elected queen,' and you will be. No one else among the seniors comes close."

"Oh, Wendy, you say that, but I don't believe it. Look at Deloris Taylor, Tiffany Huntington-Hatherford, or Cynthia Walker. They're all so gorgeous and smart, and, well . . ." She looked down and said in a small voice, "They're all close friends of Craig's."

"Well, you're gorgeous and smart, too, Dawn," Wendy retorted.

"But am I a close friend of Craig's? He doesn't even notice me. All I am to him is just another cheerleader, not an individual worth getting to know." She made a sound halfway between a laugh and a sob.

"Hey, come on, Dawn, don't cry. You know that's not true. You're not just one of the cheerleaders; you're the captain."

Dawn shook her head, her lips trembling. "Big rah-rah deal. So I'm the captain. That's even worse. That's even more like the stereotype. Ms. Grinning Bubble-Headed Queen of the Varsity. See her jump! See her lead the cheers! See her make like the little social bee with all the guys. How popular Dawn is," she intoned dramatically, "how pretty. She's got it all." Her voice wavered again. "But I don't, Wendy! I don't have the guy I really like noticing me. All the rest of it's just an act. Just a put-on to fool the other kids. I date and flirt and laugh with all the guys because I don't want the other girls to know I'm a loser. And I'm a loser because I don't have Craig."

Wendy shook her head. "Don't be ridiculous. You know Craig's been eyeing you all term."

"Oh, yes, and doing exactly what else besides eyeing? Nothing. Yet I've noticed he's been busy asking out Deloris and Cynthia and Tiffany. He may eye me, but he asks them out! Listen, Wendy, I cornered him on Friday after the game and hinted that I had something important and private to tell him. Well, I didn't really. I was going to mention the activities of the Spirit Club before the big rally on Wednesday, but he didn't know that. I made it sound very personal. Then I deliberately pretended I was in a rush and couldn't talk, and didn't call him like I said I would. And you know what this little trick accomplished? Nothing. That's right. Exactly zero. I kept thinking he'd call me or maybe even be interested enough to stop by, but no. He wasn't even interested enough to call."

Dawn's violet eyes had lost their sparkle. She looked sad and defeated. Against her better judgment, Cupid Delaney began to feel an iota of sympathy for the cheerleader's plight. Dawn wasn't just an empty-headed, empty-hearted doll with nothing more on her mind than playing games with guys, looking good, and maintaining her image. It appeared to Cupid Delaney that the girl really liked Craig and was hurt because she didn't realize her attraction was reciprocated.

And then her feelings of sympathy wavered when Dawn said softly and fiercely, "That Craig Lacrosse can't make a laughingstock out of me! I know he's going to be voted homecoming king at the dance and I've got to be his queen. You know that's what I want more than anything, Wendy. I've been planning on this for nearly four years. I've got to make it happen myself!"

There was a glitter in her eyes that frightened Cupid Delaney. She had seen pictures of voodoo doctors in *National Geographic* who had placed curses on their helpless victims with just such intensity. Dawn Cummings wanted to date Craig Lacrosse because he was a status symbol, as well as someone she liked. He also happened to be part of her grand plan. If she got Craig to escort her to the dance, her position as homecoming queen would be that much more assured.

So that was what the boy meant to her: a chance at the Grid's crown.

Well, at least now Cupid wouldn't feel too guilty about taking Craig away from Dawn's clutches. And she had learned an essential fact about her subject tonight. What others thought of Dawn Cummings was of utmost priority to her. That usually signified a somewhat shaky self-image. And Cupid Delaney knew that little bit of information was going to come in mighty handy during the next six days.

The butterfly sighed as she realized the magnitude of her assignment. She had two strange hunks on one side of the romantic equation, and she hadn't even met the other side: Helen Mapes and Alvin Danziger. If they were supposed to be thrilled to win the attention and affection of Craig and Dawn, she'd eat her hat and then start nibbling on her wings. Still, who knew what romantic fantasy lurked in the hearts of a teenage nerd and nerdette?

She'd better get going and find out.

Close Encounter of the Nerd Kind

Alvin Danziger was having a hard time talking to Helen Mapes.

Every time he opened his mouth to say something, the people at the next table shushed him. Once an irate researcher actually popped up from behind the history stacks to lay an admonishing finger to her lips.

That didn't stop Alvin. Cupid Delaney could already tell that this was a boy who did exactly as he pleased. If that's what gave him the reputation for being an oddball, then more power to him, she thought. Helen, on the other hand, kept looking down in mortification at her open book and whispering, "Alvin, please! Not so loud. We'll be thrown out."

"So what? I've always secretly dreamed of being forcibly ejected from Woodside's stuffy public library."

As if on cue, the annoyed researcher loomed around the stacks again and hissed "Quiet!", then disappeared from view.

Alvin broke into laughter, provoking louder shushes from the adjoining tables. From on top of the history stacks, Cupid Delaney got a perfect picture of the pandemonium the boy was creating and enjoying thoroughly. She had to admit the scene was pretty funny. But little Miss Bookworm, pale-faced and embarrassed, obviously didn't agree.

"Alvin, I want to go." Helen's voice was child-like but determined. There was a subtle set to her round little jaw.

Hmm. Cupid Delaney pondered. More here than meets the eye? Quiet Miss Bookworm inwardly not as docile or boring as predicted?

"Hey," Alvin protested, then, seeing her frown, lowered his voice. "The library closes at nine. We still have over twenty minutes."

"I don't care. I'm not getting anything done on this assignment, and it's clear that you don't want to work, so . . ." She snapped the book shut and began gathering her scattered papers.

Alvin watched helplessly as Helen prepared to leave and then shot out a restraining hand when she stood up. "Hey, Helen, c'mon. Don't be annoyed. I was just having fun. I'm sorry if I embarrassed you."

The prim little cast to her lips softened. "Well." She hesitated.

"Come on," he pleaded. "Don't call it quits yet. It's still pretty early and it's Saturday night. No school tomorrow. Why don't we forget about the books for a change and go back to my house and finish the game? I bet I can checkmate your king. I've been studying the board all week."

Ah, Cupid Delaney sighed. The nerd's and nerdette's notorious affinity for chess. Was that all that bound them together? Or was there more? There had to be. She could see the boy's feelings splashed all over his face. He wasn't primarily drawn to Helen Mapes for her prowess in castling or capturing pawns. It was obvious he found her attractive and wanted to be more than just a chessmate. But Cupid Delaney wasn't at all sure how Helen viewed Alvin. The readings on her romance pulsars were low indeed. The miniscule red dots in her wings acted like a Geiger counter in detecting emotional attraction between human beings. They had been glowing more dramatically around Dawn and Craig earlier, but maybe that was just because the "pretty people" generated more intrigue, excitement, and jealousy wherever they went. If you saw them on a street or in the supermarket checkout line, you'd stop and stare.

But Helen and Alvin? Well, Cupid Delaney thought, that was another story. Keeping her wings tucked in, she sidled close to the edge of the stacks and peered more intently at the couple standing below. On a scale from 1 to 10 of physical attractiveness, she would gauge Dawn and Craig to be somewhere near the 9 and 10 marks, and Helen and Alvin hovering somewhere between 3 and 4. That sounded harsh. She didn't mean it to be. Maybe Craig and Dawn zoomed to the top because they dressed so fashionably, in clothes that said, "Look at me. Check me out. I'm really something, aren't I?" Whereas Alvin and Helen blended in with the woodwork, their colors drawn from the quiet gray, dull brown, and nerd navy families.

Stop it! she admonished herself. Stop calling and thinking about them as nerds, as Valentina did. That wasn't very nice or very fair. She'd try extra hard to keep an open mind about her subjects. Wasn't that official rule number one in the *Cupid Handbook*? "A cupid must be objective toward her subjects. Partiality or emotion should not at any time present itself while the cupid is on assignment." There was more, about nineteen rules' worth, but that basically summed it up.

As if Cupid Delaney would actually flip and jeopardize her ethereal status by falling in love with a mere mortal like Alvin Danziger. The very idea was preposterous! And yet, getting right down to it, he wasn't so terribly unattractive. He was of medium height, but tending toward lean, as in string bean. He had long reddish blond hair that kids once called carrot top, worn carelessly over one eye. His boyish features and solemn expression reminded Cupid Delaney of a young Clark Kent, and his dark horn-rimmed glasses did nothing to alter this impression. Yet Cupid Delaney could sense the humor and the vulnerability lying just beneath the surface. Here was a boy who would care about someone, who would put his heart and soul on the line and not be ashamed to do so. He would make mistakes, be shy and awkward, but if he met the right girl, he'd make a wonderful boyfriend.

Cupid Delaney had no idea why or how she knew all these things about Alvin, but she did. Normally it took quite a few hours of close surveillance before getting a fix on a person, but not this time. Not for this boy. He was different. When he smiled, an appealing look came over his nearly ugly face, and he actually seemed, well, if not handsome or sexy, then decidedly cute.

Helen, on the other hand, was not cute. Although she was short, maybe five feet one or two, she was not the fragile, petite type who looked adorable in lace or ruffles. She was more the solid, athletic type, at home in jeans and a sweatshirt, with a hockey stick in her hand. The most you could say about Helen Mapes was that she was wholesome looking. Her nose was snub, her eyes were gray, her hair a tangled mass of brown curls, but she had the look of the puritan about her. Cupid Delaney pictured Dame Helen Mapes sitting in prayer meetings, a brown hood framing her face, eyes modestly downcast and resigned. On the surface.

Yes, that was it. On the surface. That was the key! That was the indefinable something Cupid Delaney sensed about the girl. Helen Mapes resignedly played the part of the colorless bookworm, but inside she rebelled. Inside, those gray eyes flashed and took half the Woodside male population by storm. Inside, the soft-spoken, shy girl got dressed up in the latest, craziest fashions and paraded proudly among the popular set. She studied all the time, but she really wanted to date, dance, and be a Dawn Cummings clone.

Oh, no, Cupid Delaney thought. This couple was in trouble. Alvin could not see the real Helen dying to get out. He had fallen for the modest, unassuming, false one. And Helen could not seriously be attracted to Alvin's type. Not if she secretly yearned to be a peer of Dawn Cummings' group. Well, that was the whole purpose behind this assignment: to make Helen and Alvin happy by having their dream dates fall in love with them. But that was going to present some difficulties. Because Cupid Delaney knew, even now, after ten minutes' surveillance, that Alvin might not harbor any concealed feelings for Dawn Cummings. She could work her magic on Dawn to have her fall for Alvin, but would Alvin succumb at all?

He *had* to, she thought. Because she was determined to complete her assignment successfully and then fly up to receive her wings.

Five minutes later Alvin and Helen stood by Alvin's car in the library parking lot. They were wavering about what to do. Cupid Delaney wished they would make up their minds. It was bitterly cold and snowflakes began to fall on the tiny butterfly shivering on the VW door handle.

"Well, if chess doesn't grab you, how about going to the Bookplate on Main, you know, that new place that sells books as well as coffee? I'd like to look at their poetry selection."

"The Bookplate?" Helen looked off into space, one foot tapping. Cupid Delaney could almost sense her desperation. Can't you see what I want? the girl seemed to be saying. I want to dance or have a party, and you're throwing more books my way. Books and a quiet cup of coffee at a small café.

When she hesitated, Alvin's face took on the helpless look Cupid had seen so many times before. Didn't Miss Bookworm, secretly Miss Party Girl, realize what she was doing to him? How he was suffering and helpless in her presence?

He blinked nervously and threw up his hands. "It's up to you, Helen. You decide. I'll go anywhere you like."

"Really?"

"Really."

"Anywhere?"

"Anywhere. You tell me."

For a moment, the girl's solemn features became animated. A spark of something—hope? excitement? anticipation?—glowed in her eyes. Was the *real* Helen Louise Mapes about to stand up?

"Well, uh, have you ever gone to Streamers?"

Alvin looked blank.

"You know," she continued, rushing through the words so that he only half heard them. "The dance club over on Aurora Avenue? The one all the kids talk about at school?"

The blank look turned into puzzlement. "What kids? I never heard anything about it."

"Oh." The glow left her face. Alvin must have noticed because he hurriedly laughed. "Hey, just because I haven't heard of Streamers doesn't make it a bad place. You know I hang out with weirdos and classified N.I.P.'s. That's Non-Important People at school. I'm just a little—surprised you suggested it. I mean, a dance club is the last place I thought you'd pick. I thought you hated blaring rock music and couldn't dance to save your life."

She's just saying that, dumbo! Cupid Delaney wanted to shout. Can't you see she's trying? It was hard enough for her to suggest Streamers without you shooting down the idea.

Helen now gave a dismissing wave of her hand and opened the car door. "It was just a crazy idea," she said, sliding into the front seat. "A joke."

"A joke?" Alvin gave a relieved laugh. "No wonder. I was—" Suddenly, out of nowhere, a flurry of colorful butterfly wings distracted his attention, and when he slid into the car, his mind went blank. He found himself saying, "Let's just drive by the place and check it out, OK?"

"OK. I mean, great, sure." Helen threw him a bewildered but pleased glance and started to hum as the VW pulled out of the lot into the street.

From the backseat of the car, behind an old issue of *Popular Mechanics* and a battered umbrella, Cupid Delaney started to hum, too, silently, and with anticipation. Timing was of the essence. In approximately four minutes, something exciting was going to happen.

Because of the snow, Alvin was taking his time and driving very cautiously, turning on Aurora as close to nine thirty as Cupid Delaney planned.

"I know I saw butterfly wings," he kept mumbling to himself. "Butterfly wings! In winter? In the snow?"

"What, Alvin?" But Helen wasn't really listening. She was eagerly searching the street for the nightclub.

"There!" she cried, spotting the sign. "Over there. And, Alvin, can you believe it? Someone's just pulling out of that space."

"Right in front of the club? Talk about luck."

Luck? Cupid Delaney pouted from the backseat. Guess again, my naive little subjects! She mentally ticked off sixty seconds as Alvin parallel parked. When she reached sixty, two things happened at once: The door to Streamers burst open and a sullen-faced Dawn came out, followed by Wendy, Tom, and two of the boys from their group; a silver Fiat screeched to a halt alongside Alvin's car, and Craig Lacrosse leaned across his date to motion that he wanted the parking space.

"What's he talking about, the jerk?" Alvin muttered, glancing at Helen. "We got here first. He'll have to find his own parking space."

But Helen wasn't responding. She was rooted to her seat, her face turned to the occupants of the silver Fiat in dreamy-eyed oblivion.

"Helen? Are you all right?" Alvin gazed at her in panic, assuming her sudden mummy state to be caused by some pain or illness. He started waving a hand in front of her drugged-looking eyes, but she impatiently pushed it away.

"I'm fine," she said, twisting around his arm to get a better view of Craig.

"No, you're not," Alvin said firmly, looking worried. "You're behaving strangely. You're breathing funny and your cheeks are all flushed."

Craig motioned again, an imperious command, for Alvin to move his VW. When the redhaired boy bared his teeth and growled, holding firm, Craig looked at first startled, then annoyed.

He leaned on his horn, blaring it, and that caught Dawn's attention.

"Craig!" she cried. She immediately stopped pouting and fixed a bright smile on her face. Then she pulled Tom close and hooked an arm possessively through his.

"Hey, man, what's going on?" the dark linebacker called. He grinned and flexed a muscle. "Is there going to be a fight?"

"Tom, stop!" Dawn protested, giggling flirtatiously for Craig's benefit. But Craig merely eyed her coldly. He was too enraged over an insubordinate's lack of respect. He leaned across to roll down the window and then glared at Alvin.

"Hey," he said, "whatever your name is—"

"Alvin Danziger." The red-haired junior bowed his head with exaggerated politeness. "And you are . . . ?"

"Craig Lacrosse," murmured Helen quickly, her shining eyes never leaving the quarterback's face.

"Never mind," snapped Craig. "I've got a movie to make and I don't have time to play Miss Manners."

"Why not?" Alvin said innocently. "It might make an interesting new pastime for you. Being polite, I mean."

The girl beside Craig shifted contemptuously. "Come on, Craig. Don't waste your time on these—these dweebs. Find another space."

Dweebs? Cupid Delaney had never heard this slang but, judging from the expression on Alvin's face, it was pretty cruel. As cruel as nerd, maybe worse. And Dawn was hopping up and down in malicious enjoyment of the performance. Craig Lacrosse being chastised by the blonde bombshell, Cynthia Walker, and failing to have his way with the oddball in the car. Oh, it was delicious. It really was. This red-haired guy—Alban, Alvin?—had to be something else to stand up to Craig so firmly. Who said "no" to Woodside's answer to hunkdom and got away with it? She eyed the VW driver more closely. A weirdo all right, and quite probably a dweeb, but tough.

Cupid Delaney watched the little scene with great relish and a certain amount of pride. In less than five minutes she had confirmed Helen's closely guarded secret and had sown the first seeds of interest in Dawn's mind for Alvin. Craig and Helen she would work on later, probably Monday at school. But the hard part was over. The romantic Achilles heel in all her subjects had been found. Now to bring the curtain down on the first act.

"Alvin," Helen whispered, biting her bottom lip. "Let's go. Let Craig have the space."

"No way. After his ridiculous behavior?"

"Please?"

Alvin stared at the girl in bewilderment. What was wrong with her? Before he could say a word, however, Craig jumped out of his sports car and strode over to the VW.

"Oh, no." Helen sank back against the seat, as if to make herself invisible.

"Hey," Tom yelled from the sidewalk. "Hey, Craig? It's not worth it. Save your energy for the game next week."

But the menacing senior was not to be deterred. Vengeance was his. And oh, how it would please him to flatten this nebbish nobody, making a fool of him in front of both Cynthia and Dawn. He flexed his fingers and approached Alvin's car door.

"Get out," he said.

"Oh, no," Helen kept babbling. "Oh, no, oh, no. Alvin, don't hurt him."

37

Alvin raised his eyebrows. "Me, hurt him? What, are you crazy? He'll kill *me*. He'll really kill me."

"Come on," Craig said. "Come on."

Cupid Delaney thought quickly. She flew up on the car seat just behind Alvin's shoulders and then perched lightly by his head. Into his ear she breathed, "Make me."

Without conscious thought, Alvin turned to meet Craig's angry face and said very clearly, "Make me."

It was said so coolly, so deliberately, that Craig took an involuntary step back. This nut Alvin was staring at him with the strangest expression in his eyes. Like he didn't know what he was going to do or say next. It was almost dangerous.

"Make me," he said again. There was something in this dweeb's fearlessness that surprised Craig. Suddenly the quarterback's mind went blank (what did he think he saw fluttering behind the redhaired guy's head?). When he came to, he looked at Alvin vacantly, then turned on his heel and got back in his car. With a roar and a slight skid, the silver Fiat drove away, leaving an amazed cast of characters behind.

Were you watching *that,* Valentina? Cupid Delaney grinned smugly. Then she took a deep breath and flew off into the night.

Cupid Reveals All

It was just another Monday morning at Woodside High. Alvin was in the school's antiquated bathroom, washing his hands and thinking about the strange events on Saturday night. Word must have gotten around about his near-wrestling match with Craig Lacrosse, because kids broke off in mid-conversation when they saw him to whisper excitedly. Big deal, Alvin thought wearily, peering at himself in the cracked mirror. Let them whisper. There wasn't much to whisper about. Craig had failed to take a swing at him and instead roared off. Alvin couldn't figure it out. He couldn't figure out a lot about that evening, including Helen's behavior as well as his own. They all seemed to be acting crazy, out of character.

He finished drying his hands and was bending down to pick up his comb when the girl popped up beside him. Popped up? Try materialized out of nowhere. He gasped and shut his eyes tightly.

This is insane, he thought. I'm imagining things. It's Monday morning and I'm in the boys' room at school and a girl cannot, repeat, can*not* be standing right next to me!

As if reading his mind, an amused voice said, "You can open your eyes now. I'm still here."

Alvin's eyes flew open. She was right. She was still there. All five feet four or so of blonde, curly hair, pink cheeks, and laughing eyes. He turned on her angrily.

"Are you crazy? Are you sick or something? This is the boys' room of the high school. Off limits to girls, or didn't you know?"

For just a second, the merriment in the girl's eyes threatened to die, but then she shrugged and giggled. "I guess I miscalculated. *Again.*"

Alvin had to admit the unexpected visitor was weird but very attractive in an unusual way. She looked about his own age, sixteen, with a sunny aura about her, all sparkle and wind chimes and charm. Her voice reminded him of the rustle of willow trees blowing in a breeze, and her incredible blue/gray/green eyes framed by the golden curls, uptilted gamine nose, and kitten smile made her resemble one of the little angels in a second-grade production of the Nativity.

And her outfit, that was weird, too. He had never seen anything like it. Not on any girl at Woodside High or at any other school, mall, or fast-food chain. Now, maybe on Halloween or at a costume party. The girl was wearing a shimmery type of pleated miniskirt with lacy white stockings and short white Robin Hood boots. Over this was a "hail, Caesar" loose-fitting blouse that fell in becoming drapes to her waist. The material was, what? Silk? Satin? Some kind of fabric that seemed to glow as she moved under the fluorescent lighting. It was unnerving and strange and very un-Monday-like activity, and *what the heck* was she doing in the boys' room at 8:50 in the morning? But her smile was incredible, warm and infectious, and he wanted to share the joke with her and be her friend. Even if being her friend meant taking her back to whatever loony bin she had escaped from or marching to the principal's office together.

He had been alone at the sink, but noise and cigarette smoke from behind the stalls brought him up short and back to reality. Any minute the door would open and someone else would come in, and then where would she be? Or him, for that matter? Entertaining a strange female in a Day-Glo tunic in a public bathroom was not honor-student behavior. And if she was a new transfer student, as he thought, she'd get in trouble, too.

"Look," he said, struggling to sound reasonable, "what are you doing in here anyway? And how'd you get in?"

Cupid Delaney raised her arms over her head for a luxurious stretch—it felt so liberating to get out of that cramped butterfly getup—and then looked around with a grin.

"Is this really the boys' bathroom?"

"No, it's the boys' cooking classroom," he retorted. "We do all our baking right over these sinks here. Of course this is the bathroom! What do you think it is?"

"I didn't know." She blinked and shook her tousled hair. "I expected to materialize in a Mr. Zenner's homeroom. I guess I'm a bit rusty."

"Rusty? You thought you'd *materialize* . . . ? No, you're not rusty. Try weird. Try a little 'Twilight Zone.' Look, whoever you are, why not avoid trouble and try materializing yourself right out of here, because the door's about to open any second and, oh, no, too late!" He turned his head at the dreaded sound of the door. A gaggle of boys burst in, laughing and talking about their weekend.

"You see?" he cried angrily, turning back to find . . . nothing. The blonde girl had gone. Just disappeared, like magic.

"What the—?" Alvin peered under the ledge and under the doors of the stalls. He scratched his head, then walked to an open window and looked out. There was not much to see, certainly not a feisty-looking girl scrambling down a rope to the ground below. There was only a bird wheeling lazily in the cloudy sky and a small, colorful butterfly flapping its wings just outside the windowsill. For a second, his mind did a wild cartwheel. A butterfly, in the freezing temperatures of late November? Why did that idea make something stir at the back of his brain? Something about Saturday night, but no. It was gone. Just like the mysterious girl.

"Looking for something, Danziger?" one of the boys asked, smirking. "Maybe a girl?"

Alvin wheeled around. "Why? Did you see her?"

The boys exchanged glances and burst out laughing. Realizing his mistake, Alvin pushed up his glasses with as much dignity as he could muster and marched to the bathroom door. As he passed the boys, he could hear snatches of conversation: ". . . Danziger with a *girl*—in here!" "Aw, the guy's a squid, you know." There was guffawing and then one shouted, "Hey, if you find your bathroom beauty, bring her to the Grid on Friday. We want to meet her."

More chuckles and rude noises. Alvin gritted his teeth and pushed open the bathroom door, to bump straight into *her:* his Robin Hoodess in white lace. Yet despite her getup, no one giggled or pointed her out. In fact, no one seemed to notice her at all!

Cupid Delaney stopped humming and smiled brightly. It was such a great smile that he almost forgot the ribbing he had just received from those

42

hyenas in there. He quickly refueled his anger and pointed a finger at her.

"You again! Now look. Enough's enough. I don't know who or what you are, what school or institution you've just floated in from, but wherever you call home, don't they teach you that a boys' bathroom is off limits to girls? Or is this your big laugh or prank for the day? A sorority or club rite or something? Because if so, you've succeeded. You've invaded an all-male area and gotten away with it. So you can go back to your club or sorority or whatever and report it's been a success. Now, kindly leave me alone."

He paused to take a breath and pushed his glasses back up again. In his excitement, they had slid down his nose. Cupid Delaney had to smile. What a character. What a speech. He looked so adorable when he was angry. His wild red hair poking out around his face, his spaniel eyes snapping. Since riling up one of her subjects was not one of her intentions, she decided to back off and calm him down. Talk to him about her mission.

"You're Alvin Danziger, aren't you?"

"Yes, sure. Why?" He frowned and took a step back, as if confronting a vampire. She shook her head and placed a gentle hand on his tense arm, grinning at the sleeve. What a difference between his sleeve and Craig's. Alvin was wearing a wrinkled plaid shirt, half pulled out at the waist and missing a button at the cuff. Craig would probably commit sartorial hara-kiri before allowing anyone at school to see him look so rumpled. His clothes had to be perfect, color-coordinated, and hermetically sealed.

"Alvin," she said softly, almost hypnotically. "I want you to listen to me. I want you to listen to me very carefully."

43

He frowned and shied away like a nervous pony, but she kept her hand on his arm.

"Listen to me," she said, locking her eyes on his. He quieted down and she smiled. "Good. No one's going to hurt you. In fact, I've come to bring you exciting news."

"Did I win the lottery or something?"

She smiled. "No, not the lottery. Something even better. Now, listen to me. Block out the sounds of everything going on around you. All right?"

He mumbled something but finally nodded. Good. He was falling under her spell. This wasn't going to be as difficult as she had anticipated.

"Now, Alvin. My name is Cupid Delaney. I've been sent here officially from the Northeastern division of the Love Bureau."

"The Love Bureau?" he said dreamily, with a vacant smile.

Cupid Delaney nodded. "That's right, Alvin. That's good. The Love Bureau. And guess what?"

"Wha-a-a-t?" Again the sleepy look and foolish grin. Cupid should have felt relieved but instead felt a jab of disappointment. Was this eccentric, outspoken boy softer-willed than she envisioned? She had pictured a real struggle between them, a clash of wills, and she realized now that her impression of her subject had been faulty. She sighed and continued.

"As an official cupid, well, an almost official one once I become certified this Friday, I've been sent down to earth to fulfill your secret dreams, Alvin. To make the girl of your fantasies fall in love with you and go to the homecoming dance with you this Friday."

His arm twitched. Cupid Delaney thought she detected a flicker of something in those dreamy brown eyes, but he grinned innocently enough and repeated, "The homecoming dance?"

Cupid Delaney nodded.

"With the girl of my dreams?"

Another nod.

"And that would be . . . ?"

"Why," she murmured, "the most beautiful, desirable, popular girl at school." (Careful, Cupid, she warned herself. Don't choke to death.) "The girl every boy would love to escort to the Grid. Dawn Cummings."

Alvin's eyes jerked open, then narrowed in disbelief.

"Dawn Cummings?"

"Er, yes." Had Valentina and the computer printouts really been correct? Did a teenage nerd always cherish the notion of dating the high school cheerleader? She felt an even bigger jolt of disappointment when Alvin leaned way back and let out a mighty roar of laughter.

"Oh, my, oh, my," he gasped, in between snorts. "I can't believe it. This is rich. This is really priceless. Me and Dawn Cummings. My secret fantasy. Taking the most popular girl at school to the Grid. Oh, oh, I'm going to explode." And off he went again, nearly causing a mini riot in the crowded hallway. Kids swarming past stopped to gaze at the spectacle of the school eccentric putting on yet another show of defiance and noncomformity.

"What a weirdo," someone muttered. "Did he say he was taking Dawn Cummings to the dance? That'll be the day."

From around the corner, the object of all this speculation came slinking seductively into view, a retinue of faithful admirers clinging to her path.

Dawn Cummings was spectacular-looking in a cream-colored, fluffy sweater and form-fitting designer jeans. The group of boys walking alongside her must have thought so, too, because each was begging her to go to the dance with him and she was laughingly debating the issue. As she approached the middle of the corridor where Alvin was still attracting attention, one of her friends came to her side.

"Dawn, that jerk Alvin Danziger is practically announcing to the whole school that he's taking you to the Grid this Friday!"

Cupid Delaney could catch the drift behind the indignant whispers, if not the actual words. As could the cluster of kids staring first at Dawn, then at Alvin. But if Alvin overheard, he didn't appear to be hurt or annoyed. He simply removed his glasses, swiped at his eyes, and then very casually straightened up. He looked directly across the jammed hallway at Dawn. Dawn began to utter a rude remark until she caught sight of the red-haired boy.

It was him! That dweeb who had stood up to Craig on Saturday night and lived to tell the tale. Alvin Danziger. She had never noticed him before—why should she? A sun can't shine on *every* star in its galaxy—but now she took the time to file him away in her mental Rolodex of weird but oddly attractive boys. Boys she would never dream of dating, let alone be seen talking to, but who still would be fun to speculate about whenever she got bored with her current crop of boyfriends. She thought all this in the split second before her friend's outraged comment and recognizing Alvin. She was going to sweep past the whole situation as if it were below her, when she felt her feet turn and begin to march quite resolutely up to the nerd! Oh, no, what was she doing? Why were her feet obeying the sound of a different drummer and bringing her to certain social ruin?

Cupid Delaney screwed up her forehead and continued to concentrate. "Come on," she whispered. "Just six more steps. You can do it." Then she mentally cheered as Dawn edged her way through the crowd to Alvin as easily and as dramatically as Moses parting the Red Sea.

"Here she is," Cupid murmured to Alvin. "Your dream girl." Had she disguised the note of sarcasm in her voice?

Alvin quickly turned to Cupid, the vacant look gone from his face completely. He bent over and hissed, "All right, joke's over, Easter Bunny. I played along for a little while, but it's not funny anymore. Not when you bring someone as dense, as plastic, as Dawn Cummings into it. Dream girl? Maybe for a Cro-Magnon man with a dinosaur brain, but not for me. The only girl I go for is the one who's just come through the door down there. And I don't need the services of some screwed-up matchmaker passing herself off as a cupid. A cupid, for gosh sake! How insipid can you be? Why not play Santa Claus, or a fairy godmother for that matter? That's pretty funny, but the joke's over. You've had your laugh, but this is where it ends."

Cupid Delaney could only stare at the boy as he delivered this tirade and then watch him turn his back on a mortified Dawn.

First, Alvin Danziger was talking out loud to himself, like some nut case, the cheerleader thought. Then he was ignoring her. Ignoring *her*, only the High Priestess of Fashion and Relationships at Woodside. Dawn stood staring at the back of his head as he raised his hand and called out, "Helen! Hey, wait up!" This carrot-topped slug was turning his back on her to wave at some mouse who had just scuttled in through the side entrance. Helen, was that her name? She looked like a Helen, old-fashioned and out of step, with the wrong hairstyle, no makeup, and the worst outfit to hit the school since "Little House on the Prairie" had a rummage sale.

Cupid Delaney, too, was as bewildered and as annoyed as Dawn. To think that this boy—no, this subject—would actually lie to her, pretend to be falling under her spell, and then fling it back in her face. She prayed that Valentina or the other Sweetheart Squad leaders had failed to monitor her actions. If not, she'd be in for a talking to that would make her bow and arrows spin, and the mission was on shaky enough ground as it was. No, she had to succeed this week. She *had* to. And Alvin was not going to prevent her from achieving her dream and getting her wings. He couldn't stop her. He'd have to succumb sooner or later.

While a sullen-faced Dawn slunk away in defeat, Cupid Delaney hurriedly caught Alvin's arm. "Listen," she said, her voice low and intense, "you can believe anything you want, but I *am* a real cupid. And no one can see me or hear me except you. There really is a Love Bureau and you *are* going to go to the Grid with the girl of your dreams."

"Then it better be Helen Mapes," he snapped. "Because she's the only one I plan to take."

He peered at Cupid Delaney over the rims of his glasses, giving her a challenging yet pitying look. "No one can see you or hear you? I almost feel sorry for you, poor kid. You don't know when to end a joke."

Cupid Delaney's sunny disposition was slowly turning cloudy. "It's no joke, I can assure you." She smiled coolly. "I really am an invisible cupid. And I have the powers to prove it."

48

Alvin rolled his eyes. "Oh, sure. Now we're talking powers. OK. How?"

"Meet me at the football field after school. Right after school, understand?"

Her lower lip trembled, but she kept her chin up.

"Wow, you're something else, Easter Bunny." He grinned. "You've got guts, I've got to admit. All right, I'll meet you on the field at three. But if you're planning on inviting the Tooth Fairy or Tinker Bell or any of your other magical friends, count me out. I can only cope with you."

"Ha, ha." Cupid Delaney watched Alvin give her a dismissing wave and then hurry down the hall to catch up with Helen. *If that's his dream girl, I'm really in trouble,* she thought. *This is going to be harder than I envisioned.* Yet deep down, in some part of her furiously beating heart, she realized she was excited, as well as angry and determined. The ugly/attractive boy had one of the strongest wills she had ever encountered, and to lock horns (and hearts) with him was going to prove a tough challenge—and maybe fun?

Hmmm, she thought, *I wonder if the Tooth Fairy is free this afternoon.*

The Quarterback
Makes a Pass
at the Bookworm

Cupid Delaney had done her homework.

When the first bell rang at 2:40, she knew exactly where each of her four subjects would be. She had to. In order to make her daring plan succeed, the timing and execution had to be perfect. Groaning a little as she returned to butterfly form, she winged her way to Mr. Palmeri's English class. The short, bearded teacher had just dismissed his students, and Alvin was edging over to where Helen was gathering up her books. They looked a little nervously at each other and both began speaking at once.

"Listen, about our plans . . ." Alvin began.

"Something's come up and . . ." Helen said at the same time.

They stopped and began to laugh.

"You first." Alvin grinned.

"No, tell me what you were going to say." Helen smiled back at him, but even from the distance of the blackboard, Cupid Delaney could tell the girl appeared uneasy.

Alvin nodded. "All right. About our plans this afternoon to study in the library? I have to cancel. I can't explain right now, but I've got to be somewhere at three. And don't ask me where, because if I told you, you wouldn't believe it. But I've got to take care of it. Is breaking our date all right with you?"

"You can't make it?" Helen's nervousness had fled in a second. She looked relieved. "That's great. I mean, that's a shame. I guess I'll have to wade through the stacks alone."

"But I thought you started to say before that something's come up? Did you have other plans?"

"Me? No!" She shook her head too quickly, an idiotic grin on her face. "No, Alvin, you must have misunderstood me. I forgot what I was saying. It had to do with the assignment, I bet. Can you believe Mr. Palmeri is asking us to read both those short stories in one evening? And then write a paper the same night? Why, both those stories run well over ten pages and . . ."

She was babbling. And Alvin was buying her story. Were all boys so naive? Cupid Delaney thought not. She knew where Helen was going at three o'clock, and it wasn't to the library. With a sigh, she spread her wings and took off for the boys' gym.

"So who's the King of the Hop taking to the big dance on Friday? Or will that require a multiple-choice answer?"

There was good-natured laughter in the crowded locker room and Craig joined in. He finished lacing up his athletic shoes, dusted off the cleats, and then slammed the locker shut.

"Can't give away trade secrets, man," he said. "Lacrosse love techniques have been passed down in our family generation after generation. They're not merely tips, but tradition. A way of life."

"Oh, no, listen to him," Tom Delacruz said. "I still think you should share the wealth."

The other members of the Pirates football team shouted their agreement in somewhat off-color terms, but Craig only shook his head.

"No way. I've worked too hard to give it away. You all know that."

"Modesty, thy name sure ain't Lacrosse!" Tom said, laughing. He picked up his helmet, then tossed Craig's over. The quarterback caught it easily and followed Tom and the rest of the team from the gym into the cold November air.

Coach Dunbarton stood by the open door and barked, "Let's go! Let's move! Let's make those bodies mean machines out there today! Delacruz!" He eyed the linebacker with a scowl. "No more goofing off like on Saturday. I'm watching you."

Tom turned to Craig and grimaced. "What put him in such a good mood? He's been jumping down our throats since last week. And he's acting like this practice today is for real."

"He's psyched," Craig said. "What can I tell you? The big championship game's only three days away and if we lose, he's going to take the heat. You can't blame him. Woodside hasn't lost a homecoming game to West Orange in eight years. And he doesn't want to start now."

When Tom and Craig began to analyze West Orange's chances for an upset victory, Cupid Delaney tuned out. Enough macho talk was enough. As it was, her hiding place inside Craig's helmet was giving her motion sickness, what with the rocking motion it made dangling carelessly from the boy's hand.

The lovebirds were all converging on one spot. It was almost time for her first big show of power. Flapping her wings, Cupid Delaney flew straight out of Craig's helmet like a freshly popped champagne cork and prayed no one would notice her. No one did. They were all too engrossed in discussing new plays. Cupid Delaney left them and soared high overhead, searching in vain for her two other subjects. Alvin was nowhere in sight, but Dawn had just run into the stadium, looking even more come-hither than ever in the Woodside varsity cheerleader uniform. She was surrounded by giggling junior- and senior-level cheerleaders, all decked out in the short, swirling skirt and heavy pullover sweater, a large black *P* emblazoned on the front.

Cupid immediately made a beeline for the girl, especially since Craig had paused to talk to her. Preening and nervously fluffing her hair, Dawn returned Craig's casual greeting. She was all too aware that this would be the perfect opportunity to repair the damage to her ego from being ignored by that dweeb Alvin.

"I voted for you this morning," she plunged in, and then blushed. Whatever had possessed her to lose her cool like that and blurt out something so adolescent? But Craig chuckled, seemingly pleased by the remark.

"You did? Well, that's great. I could use every vote I can get, believe me."

As if Mr. Big, class hunk, would ever have to worry his shiny golden head about being elected homecoming king. Cupid Delaney needed to get closer and located the perfect spot to camouflage herself—Dawn's large, tasseled pompom, which was lying on the ground right next to the couple.

Wendy Chu and several other cheerleaders had drifted over to the magical couple, and now Tom Delacruz and some members of the team attached themselves to the group.

"Ah, who did you vote for?" Good going, Dawn baby. Don't let the Sun King walk away without divulging any secrets.

Craig looked a little taken aback. He smiled and shook his head. "That's privileged information."

Dawn poked Craig playfully. "That's not fair! I admitted I cast my vote for you. The least you can do is tell me who you voted for."

Tom joined in. "She's right, Craig. We're all just dying to know . . ."—he mock slid to the ground—"so tell us who you want your homecoming queen to be. After all, you're a shoo-in for king."

"Yeah, come on, Lacrosse," another friend urged. "Quit holding out on us."

Cupid Delaney screwed her eyes shut and concentrated. As Dawn held her breath, waiting to hear her own name spoken, Craig hesitated. He blinked once, stared into the bleachers, and declared, "There, that girl sitting by C section. That's who I voted for."

There was an odd glint in his eyes, but Dawn didn't notice. She was too busy staring at the person he had named.

"Her? Helen whatever-her-name-is, the little mouse?" Her mouth fell open. "I don't believe it!"

"Why, who is she?" Wendy gazed first at Craig and then at Dawn in bewilderment. Everyone in the group immediately turned to stare en masse at Helen, who blushed bright crimson and tried to shrink even further back along the stadium wall. She couldn't hear everything they were saying, but just enough to catch her name and the mention of homecoming queen. And they all were examining her in disbelief. Like someone had just yanked a sheet off her head and announced: "Ladies and gentlemen of the press, I introduce to you the first Martian in captivity!" Only Craig's expression was different. He had this innocent and sweet smile and he was winking directly at her and so what if the rest of them were staring at her, whispering about her, she didn't care, *he* was noticing her, wasn't he? *He* was looking at her for the first time she could ever remember and seeing her as a person, not the invisible blob she always thought she was at school. Let the cheerleaders gawk and the big dumb jocks stare, too. It didn't matter. Nothing mattered except for the fact that her idol, Craig Lacrosse, had noticed her and smiled and winked at her. And that made all her secret trips to his football games and after-school practices and student government meetings worthwhile.

Helen averted her eyes and tried to control her wildly thumping heart.

"Oh, come on!" Dawn burst out, stamping her foot angrily. "You wouldn't possibly nominate that— that 1970s creature to be the queen."

Tom scratched his head. "What 1970s creature? Fill me in."

Craig didn't hear the question. He was too busy staring at the mysterious girl he had selected on a whim. He guessed it had been a whim. He couldn't figure out why he had chosen who he did. But now her identity was coming back to him, the girl's voice, her face. Saturday night in front of Streamers. She had been in the car with that strange red-haired creep. What was his name? Almost magically it came to him.

"Albert or Alvin Danziger," he announced, staring mesmerized into the bleacher section. "The girl goes out with him. Her name is Helen; isn't that what you said, Dawn?"

Dawn frowned. "Yes, but honestly, Craig, you've got to be kidding!"

"Why?" he asked. "I think she's kind of cute."

While Dawn and Wendy exchanged horrified glances, Tom clapped a hand on his friend's shoulder. "She's not exactly my idea of hot-date bait, but I guess the joke's on us. You really have these girls here believing your story!"

Everyone cracked up, including a visibly relieved Dawn, who laughed harder than anyone else at Craig's supposed leg-pulling. But no one heard Craig whisper, "What story? I think Helen is beautiful."

Helen, highly mortified now by all the laughter and giggling wafting her way, tried to escape. But Coach Dunbarton strode over to where she was standing and unknowingly blocked her escape.

"All right, break it up!" he snarled. "This isn't play school. This is a practice. An important one, or did you all forget? Dawn! Get your cheerleaders off to the side and clear the field. And all you meatheads, quit clowning around and get to work. I want to see some sweat out there. We got three new plays to work on. Now let's go! Let's move!" He blew his whistle, and mercifully the jeering and the laughter stopped. Craig blinked, shook his head as if clearing it, and then quietly motioned to Dawn.

"I want to see you later," he said and then ran confidently out on the field. Dawn did a buoyant cartwheel. This was *it*! Invitation time. She knew he had been teasing about Helen!

Enough, the butterfly thought. Poor Helen has had it. But don't you worry, Helen, your turn up at bat is coming next! And with her own private chuckle, she stretched her wings and soared off behind the stadium. Time to play Clark Kent and switch back to her corporeal state and finally knock some sense into Alvin.

"Will you kindly stop doing that?" the red-haired boy snapped seconds later as Cupid Delaney popped up by his side at the stadium entrance. "You're going to give me a heart attack at the age of sixteen with your jack-in-the-box impressions. Or should I say *cupid* impressions? All right. You've coerced me into meeting you here, but I don't understand any of it."

"Oh, you will," she promised him gaily. Now that Alvin had shown up, her sour mood had improved. There was something *intriguing* about the boy, something bright and intelligent she found herself liking.

"Follow me," she instructed Alvin. He grumbled but fell into step beside her until they reached the middle of the sideline. There she stopped, and then pointed a dramatic finger toward the center of the field where a practice game was beginning.

"Observe Craig," she said quietly. The blond boy was bent over in a huddle, obviously calling the plays.

"Yeah, yeah, the big quarterback." Alvin threw up his hands in disgust. "So what?"

"So what?" Cupid Delaney asked with a naughty grin on her face. "So—*this*."

She screwed up her forehead, murmured something, then pointed a dramatic finger at Craig. She didn't cry "Shazaam," Alvin would have later sworn, but it sounded very close. All at once, the quarterback stopped, mid-play. While the defense rushed him, he gazed wildly around the field and then at the stands and was brought down with grunts where he stood.

There was stunned silence on the field. Off on the sideline, Coach Dunbarton blew his whistle. "What's going on out there? Lacrosse, get with it, no hesitation next time. Now, get back to do the play again, but this time get rid of the ball fast. Carter's going to be waiting for your pass. OK, let's go!"

The players took their places, but Craig walked slowly, almost unsurely, to the huddle. His gaze never left the stands, where an embarrassed but mesmerized Helen sat. A few of the cheerleaders commented about this strange behavior, but Dawn shushed them. No one better say anything negative about her date to the Grid. She was confident Craig's loss of attention had to do with her. He was probably rehearsing what he was going to say to her, to ask her to the dance.

Cupid Delaney eyed Alvin. He returned her gaze coolly.

"Well?"

"Well, what?" Alvin said. "Craig makes a mistake. So what?"

Cupid Delaney sighed. "A mistake? I don't perform mistakes. Just keep your eye on the quarterback."

Lowering her head, she closed her eyes and mumbled a few words that were inaudible to Alvin. Again the eyes opened, the finger pointed, and she whispered what sounded like "Shazaam."

This time Craig didn't stop once the play was called. He tossed the ball high in the air, caught it with a gleeful laugh, and then skipped with it toward the goalposts—the goalposts in the wrong direction.

Everyone on the field stood still, muttering among themselves. What in the world was going on? What was he doing? A practical joke was fine every once in a while, in the locker room or after practice, but never, *never* during a play. And never when Coach Dunbarton was supervising the action, his eyebrows now bristling in rage.

"Lacrosse!" he roared. "Get over here, fast!"

But Craig had other ideas. He sketched a jaunty salute to the coach and turned away. He jogged over to the stadium bleachers where Helen sat, huddled inside her polo coat, her snub nose pink from the cold and from embarrassment. Now her nose was becoming redder, as was the rest of her face, when Craig bounded up the rows and came to a stop in front of her.

"What is he doing?" Wendy whispered to Dawn. "Why is he acting so crazy?"

Dawn shook her head slowly. "I don't know. It's a joke, I think. He's still pretending he's nuts about Helen."

"Hey, what's going on?" Alvin turned uneasily to Cupid Delaney, but she was too elated to notice. She was following Craig's behavior with close attention, whispering, "I did it! I really did it."

"Did what?" Alvin's tone was sharp, but only because he was beginning to get the strangest feeling that this crazy, blue-eyed "witch" really had done something. And Craig was under her spell. Why else would the star quarterback foul up an important practice and risk getting thrown off the team? And why would the school's Mr. Cool now be intently talking to that scared little girl in the stands, the one in the coat and scarf who looked so much like—

"Helen! That's Helen up there!" he cried. He turned indignantly. "How does she come into this? Did you plant her here, too, make her materialize or whatever you call it in Cupid Land?"

"It's the Love Bureau, and no, I swear to you, I had nothing to do with Helen's being here. She planned that all on her own."

"But, but—she told me she was going to study in the library today. I don't understand it." Alvin looked over at Helen and Craig, his eyes behind the glasses vulnerable and questioning.

"Maybe you should ask her." Her tone was light, but she had to crush her impulse to reverse the spell and erase the bewildered, hurt look on Alvin's face. She was allowing her own emotions to interfere with the mission, and she couldn't, *wouldn't* let herself do that. The mission came first. Her flying up to become a certified cupid was her number-one dream. And to do that, she had to step on her subjects' toes.

"Maybe I will ask Helen," Alvin said. "But I'm still not totally convinced you're a real, live cupid. Just because Craig's making a fool of himself doesn't prove anything to me."

"Suit yourself." Cupid Delaney winked at him, then—snap!—turned into a delicate butterfly, fluttering before his astonished face.

"Hey! Did you see *that*?" he called out to nearby cheerleaders, but they shrugged and looked at him like he was crazy. This girl really was invisible to everyone but him!

"Wait! Wait, I take it back," he cried, but it was too late. She was needed elsewhere. The little butterfly circled his body, then darted over to the stands, where a distressed Craig was still pleading with Helen.

"I'm serious," he kept saying. "I really am. I want you to go out with me, get to know me. Please, Helen, say yes. Please?"

Helen couldn't get a word out. Her throat was locked and she was on the verge of tears. How much more could she take? It was really too much. First hearing jokes about her being nominated for homecoming queen and now this full frontal attack by the boy of her dreams. He had never noticed her before. So why was he being so cruel and pretending he was infatuated with her? It didn't make sense. It was mean and heartless and a big joke and yet, as much as she tried, she could not hate him. She could never hate someone so beautiful, so nearly godlike as Craig Lacrosse. With a tiny whimpering sound, she jumped up and clattered down the steps to the exit.

Craig wheeled around and shouted, "Helen! Wait. I adore you! Please come back. Please!"

Helen threw one last mortified look behind her as she reached the exit and ran out. Craig raced down the bleachers, shouting, "Helen! Wait! Come back!"

Cupid Delaney witnessed the disbelief on the faces of all the people watching the scene. One, however, was laughing.

"Oh, Lord, he's so crazy, it's hysterical," Dawn was saying to Wendy and the girls on her squad. "Craig's still putting on an act. It's a joke, for heaven's sake. A joke! Can't you all see that?"

Alvin overheard the words as he slowly, dispiritedly walked past the cheerleaders. He remembered the scene in the boys' bathroom that morning, the inconspicuous butterfly perched on the window ledge. He played back the confrontation with Craig Saturday night in front of Streamers. Hadn't there been something about a butterfly distracting him? And Craig's amazing about-face. By rights Alvin should have been decked thoroughly by Craig. But what happened? Craig's fury had dissipated into a blank stare, and he had simply walked away. All these pieces assembled together made a very disturbing picture. Yes, Virginia, he thought, there really is a Cupid. And knowing that, Craig's sudden obsession with Helen was no joke or prank to be laughed away as Dawn was doing.

For the first time, Alvin felt scared. If this Cupid Delaney was as powerful as he thought she was, all the students of Woodside High were in danger of losing their hearts. Or was it just going to be Helen, Craig, and him? She won't get away with it, he vowed. I'll boycott Valentine's Day if I have to. Feeling a little better, and actually managing a grin, he went in search of Helen.

The Hunk Succumbs

"Helen, dear, he's out there again and I really think you should talk to him."

"No."

"But he's been sitting out front so patiently and it's just started to rain."

"I don't care if it's raining. I don't care if it's hailing. I refuse to talk to him."

Helen pushed back from the table, her bowl of oatmeal half-eaten. Chloris Mapes, a faded woman in her late thirties, threw a pleading look at her husband, but he raised an eyebrow and continued to read the paper. Helen's two sisters, Dorothy, fourteen, and Ethel, twelve, burst into the kitchen like falling meteors.

"He's out there, Helen, sitting in that sexy silver car of his—"

"Dorothy!" reproved Mrs. Mapes, but bubbling Dorothy couldn't be restrained.

"Well, it *is* sexy, you know it is, and so is he! Oh, Craig Lacrosse has to be the sexiest male in Woodside, he's awesome, he really is, and to think he's been asking you out, well, I can't believe it, I really can't."

"Well, don't start believing it," Helen snapped. "It's all just a game, a really stupid joke. Craig would never seriously ask me out on a date, not in a million years."

"But all my friends are talking about it. They say Craig went all goofy yesterday afternoon at practice and went dancing down the field and Coach Dunbarton had a fit, he nearly suspended Craig, and Craig chased you all over the bleachers and—"

"He did not!" Helen cried, blushing crimson.

"He did, too!"

"Wow." Ethel gazed at Helen with admiration. "I didn't know that part. Did he catch you, Helen?"

"No, he did not catch me, and he's not going to. He doesn't really want to. It's just a silly game he's playing, and he doesn't really like me at all. Now, I have to get to school and I don't want to be late. So you can all stop holding your breath about me and Craig Lacrosse. You and the whole stupid school!"

"But then why did Craig keep calling her, all yesterday afternoon and last night?" Dorothy asked, but Mrs. Mapes shushed her and Helen stormed out, failing to notice a tiny butterfly in her oversized cardigan pocket. Cupid Delaney hopped up and down in excitement in the dark wool cave. Things were going beautifully. She was right on schedule. Monday she had cast the net of her romantic powers over Craig. The fish had swallowed the bait and fallen head over heels for Helen Mapes. Today she would have to show Dawn that Craig's calflike behavior was not a joke. Once Dawn saw the light, Cupid would place Alvin in her path. Not that the ornery red-haired boy would fall all over himself to ask Dawn to the Grid. And not that Dawn would accept at this point. That part was going to take a bit of work. But she had the skills and determination to complete this mission, and nothing was going to stop her.

"Hang in there, Helen," she whispered from the depths of the sweater pocket. "In a day or two you're going to realize Craig is seriously gone on you and then won't your ego get a boost!" As Helen reached into the hall closet to extract an umbrella, Cupid Delaney edged out of her hiding place. Time to play nurse with the Incredible Hunk and take his romantic temperature.

Craig sat huddled inside the Fiat, peering through the rain at the house. It was cold in the car, and tiny drops of water kept sliding through the half-cracked window to plop on his leg, but he didn't notice. All his energy and concentration were focused on 622 Long Oak Road. Any minute *she* would open the door and walk into his field of vision. He would be able to look at her again, really see her, and not sit back, eyes closed, trying in vain to recall her features. That had kept him awake last night. When he finally dozed off, tired and miserable, he had dreamt about her. What was going on? he wondered. Why were all his waking, and even sleeping, thoughts of a small, solid-looking girl with a red nose and captivating gray eyes? She wasn't his type. Man, was she ever *not*. She wasn't tall or glamorous. She wasn't flirtatious, sexy, or even attractive. And that voice. Like Goldilocks or something, high-pitched, thin, childish. He thumped his knee with an angry fist. What was wrong with him? Was he slipping mental gears or under too much stress? Maybe that fall he took at the game two weeks ago had jarred more than his trick knee. He wasn't behaving like the smooth old operator he was, that's for sure. And everyone was starting to notice.

Let them, he thought in the next breath, as the door opened and *she* appeared. Oh, she was wonderful. She was a dream. He sucked in his breath and pressed his nose against the window. Cupid Delaney lay perfectly flat and still against the back of the headrest and smothered a giggle. If only Craig could see himself now, she thought. What a picture. The school's most handsome senior, with his face pressed to the glass like a little puppy at a pet store. And he was gazing at Helen just like a puppy, too, with quivering admiration and unlimited devotion. If he had a tail, he'd be wagging it, Cupid Delaney thought. She had to remind herself to cut the jokes or she'd really go off into giggles, then her wings would start flapping and Craig might notice.

"Helen," he whispered.

The girl hurriedly opened her umbrella, shifted her books more closely to her chest, and took off down her front steps at a fast clip. Not once did she look at the car parked across the street from her house.

Craig yanked down his window. "Helen! Hey, Helen, please wait a minute?"

The girl in the little yellow raincoat hesitated. A face, pale, hurt, looked across at him, then away. She shook her head and kept walking.

"Helen!"

Craig gunned the motor, turned the car around, and followed her down the street. When she stopped at the corner, he leaned his head out.

"At least let me give you a ride to school. The rain's getting worse."

Helen ignored the offer. She crossed the street and flagged down the school bus as it lumbered to a halt. Merging with the rest of the kids who jumped on board, she soon became lost to Craig. That didn't stop the lovesick puppy. Muttering under his breath, he pulled alongside the bus and scanned all the windows. There! In the middle row, by the outside window. There was the girl who had gotten so mysteriously under his skin.

"Helen," he murmured. He tapped the horn and leaned across the car. Some of the kids looked out.

"Get Helen," he mouthed and pointed.

They stared at him and exchanged smirking glances.

"What's wrong with those oafs?" Craig burst out. He touched the horn, harder and longer. Helen peered out once, her lips rounding into a horrified O, then drew her head back in like a turtle.

"Helen!" Craig cried. He leaned his head across and rolled down the passenger-seat window. "Helen! I want to talk to you! Get off the bus!"

The school bus swung its door shut and pulled out into traffic.

Quickly, his hands fumbling with the gearshift, Craig shot ahead, following the bus its half-mile route. The whole time Helen kept her shoulders hunched, her face turned away from the window.

Craig didn't let up. He had seen the light. His girl-chasing days—plural—were over. There was only one girl he wanted to chase now, and he had to catch her. Catch her and take her to the Grid with him.

Craig started when he realized he had been sitting behind the school bus at Woodside. Frantically, he checked the bus, but Helen had disappeared. She had probably slipped off first to avoid him. Craig cursed under his breath and hit the wheel. Was she always going to elude him? And then Craig had his brainstorm. Actually, Cupid Delaney thought smugly, she had the brainstorm and just passed it on to him. It occurred to her when she spotted Dawn and Wendy walking into the main entrance. Cupid knew that Dawn was the founder and president of the newly formed activities committee at school, informally called the Spirit Club. As prestigious and socially high-ranking as the varsity cheering squad or the football team, the small group ultimately wanted to enlist ten members—five outgoing, popular girls, school leaders, and likewise, five energetic guys, the movers and shakers in student government and athletics. Dawn was the founder and president and was so far chief selection board for the closed, elite organization. Naturally, Wendy Chu had met the requirements, as had Tom Delacruz and Craig Lacrosse. The Holy Four had so far been supplemented by three other males—yearbook and newspaper editors—but only two other girls had been voted in. There was one more opening to fill. With the big homecoming game coming up in two days and school spirit running high, Cupid Delaney realized that now would be a perfect time to fill that vacancy. And she knew exactly who would fit the bill. For all romantic purposes, that is.

"The Spirit Club," Craig announced suddenly in the silence of the car. "The Spirit Club, that's it! I'll make Dawn nominate Helen, and with my backing and the votes of Tom and the other guys, she'll get in. And then I'll have the chance to talk to her and let her see I'm serious about her. She'll get in. I know she will."

It was a brilliant idea and he was proud of himself. Cupid Delaney rolled her eyes, but allowed the boy to take all the credit. She didn't want Craig or Dawn or even Helen to realize an outside force was controlling their actions. No, it was working perfectly just as it was, Craig gone bonkers over Helen and now plotting to draw the shy little mouse into the rarified social hierarchy of Woodside High. It would raise eyebrows. It would ruffle feathers, Dawn's and Alvin's to be exact, but so what? It would get the love ball rolling, and that's all Cupid Delaney needed.

Alvin and Cupid Get on
the Right Track

Dawn eyed the order of fries with distaste, but she picked one up and nibbled at it. Outwardly she appeared happy and in control. Inwardly she was seething. She was sitting in the back booth of Friendly's, the school's favorite hangout, which was noted for its extraordinary shakes and sundaes, but this afternoon she was in no mood for any gooey concoction. Nor for the french fries and Diet Coke she had ordered to keep up appearances. Mustn't let her friends think what had just transpired had fazed her in the least.

She swallowed the tasteless fry and quickly sipped her drink. How was she going to get through an hour or more of this pretense? All her friends laughing and chattering and demanding to hear more about the episode with Craig. And she, wanting more than anything else in the world to forget it.

"So give us more dirt," pleaded Claire Reggio, a big name in Drama Club and a member of the Spirit Club. Her green eyes glistened with curiosity.

"Yeah, come *on*, Cummings," Wendy said. "Quit playing with those french fries and talk to us.

Craig couldn't be serious about nominating that Helen Apes—"

"Mapes."

"—Mapes character for our Spirit Club. I mean, it's unreal. A fairy tale."

Tell me about it, Dawn thought bitterly. *Fairy tale* was too nice a word for what was happening to her world right now. Unless it was the Brothers Grimm and then they'd have to change their name to Gruesome. Oh, it was gruesome all right. But she had to keep it in. Smile and lie and pretend everything was fine, all for the sake of saving face.

She ran a careless hand through her hair.

"Well, Craig's right in a way. We really should open up the club to different grades. I mean, as it is, we're all seniors. Who's going to know how to run the organization once we graduate?"

Wendy leaned back with a snort. "Tell us another one. I hardly think a club like ours needs a blueprint. Come on, Dawn! Why did Craig force you into nominating that nobody?"

"He didn't force me."

"Oh, you volunteered all on your own?"

Claire and Wendy stared at Dawn, and she felt her poise slipping. Honestly, how much longer could she keep this up? These girls were her closest friends, her best friends really, and pretending Craig's bombshell hadn't shocked and hurt her was more than she could take.

"All right," she said in a small, defeated whisper. "He did force me. He made me agree to ask Helen to join us for the big pregame meeting of the Spirit Club tomorrow."

"The party at your place? I don't believe it!"

Dawn gave a sharp, impatient motion of her head. "Well, you'd better start. I already talked to Helen, right after school, and invited her. She was

71

simply awestruck. She just stood there, beaming like an idiot at me. And that voice of hers. Honestly, you've got to hear it to believe it. 'Oh, you mean you're asking me, little old me, to be in the Spirit Club?'" Dawn mimicked, her voice a childish lisp.

"Oh, come on."

"I'm serious. Shirley Temple lives and breathes again, and she's reincarnated in the bloblike form of Helen Mapes."

Clare giggled but was shot a warning look by Wendy and turned her laugh into a cough.

"But why did Craig nominate her?" Wendy persisted.

Dawn nibbled at a perfectly manicured nail. "If I understood the reason behind that 64,000 Dollar Question, I'd be rich and in Tahiti right now. *I don't know*. It's driving me crazy. I have no idea what he sees in her, I honestly don't."

"But he sees something?" Wendy said softly, slowly.

Dawn nodded, too miserable and enraged to trust herself to speak.

Claire looked across at Wendy and raised a shoulder. "You think it's a joke? Like yesterday at practice?"

"Forget it," Dawn snapped. "That's what I told myself, and look what a fool I've been. That was no joke, Craig running off the field to talk to Helen in the bleachers. He was serious."

"That's not serious. That's sick."

"Yeah, well, you may be right, but what can we do about it *now* is what I need to know. Yes, I told Craig I'd ask Helen to join us at the Spirit Club meeting tomorrow, but I didn't promise him she'd get in. I mean, what credentials does she have? We're all active in school; we've run committees and set up dances and fund raisers and plays, but the mouse? Don't make me laugh."

Claire stared off into space for a few moments, an abstracted look in her eyes. Then she thumped the table. So vehement was her action that no one noticed a tiny butterfly as it toppled off the back of a saltshaker. Exposed and frantic, Cupid Delaney lay on the table, too stunned to move. Just as she spotted her escape route, behind the napkin holder, Dawn looked down.

"Oh, look out!" she squealed. "A bug!"

She flapped her hands and Wendy began shrieking. "Get it! Get it! It's going to go on your french fries!"

Cupid Delaney wanted nothing more at this point than to stop, call time out, and set these twittering schoolgirls straight. She wanted to tell them that she was not a common bug; she was a representative of the highly beautiful diurnal lepidopterous family. And as such, did not resort to such low tactics as dive-bombing french fries or attacking overly dramatic girls.

But who had the time? Her life was at stake. Already Dawn had pulled out a straw and was jabbing at her.

"Get it!" Wendy kept shrieking, cowering behind the large menu. And Claire was ignoring the whole "Wild Kingdom" scenario to thump the table repeatedly and announce: "That's it! I've got it! The perfect way to boot Helen out."

Whatever her plan was, Cupid Delaney was not destined to find out. Feinting and tripping over her legs, and trying to avoid her attacker's jabs, she was almost ready to message for help. But rescue came, not from the Love Bureau, but from an all-too-human source.

"What's all the hysterics about?"

The voice was irritated and yet anxious. Dawn swung around and frowned at Alvin.

"Isn't it obvious? This—this thing is scaring us to death!"

"Or the other way round, I bet." He quickly leaned across the booth and pulled the straw from her hand.

"Hey!"

"Hey, nothing. The way you were going on, you'd think you were doing battle with Mothra. This little creature, if you'd happen to notice, is a butterfly. A harmless butterfly. Now let it alone."

Alvin pulled out a handkerchief and gently scooped a dazed Cupid Delaney onto it. Muttering to himself, he examined the body for possible injury and, satisfied there was none, gently knotted the handkerchief, and turned to leave.

"Well, wait a moment," Dawn called. "You don't have to act like I'm a cold-blooded killer or something. That thing just scared us, that's all. I didn't meant to hurt it."

Why was she delaying him, apologizing for her actions? As if it mattered what this carrot top thought of her?

But Alvin had no time for the girl. Her silly behavior only strengthened his resolve not to fall under Cupid Delaney's spell and wind up taking the cheerleader to the dance. No, if he was going at all, and he wanted to, Helen would be at his side. But first he had a bone to pick with a certain little cupid, the one who was tied up quite securely in the handkerchief. No pulling her disappearing act on him this time. Not before he had his say.

He cut off Dawn in midstream and left the restaurant. It was damp and raw on the street. A cold wind knifed through his coat and he adjusted his scarf. The knotted handkerchief in his hand twitched, and he grinned. He raised the white cloth to his mouth and said, softly yet distinctly, "Yes, I know you want to get out. And you will, very shortly, but you've got to promise me you won't fly away or disappear."

He carefully untied one of the knots and peered in. Cupid Delaney stared back at him, two beady black eyes snapping in anger. Her wings were opening and closing with increasing determination and energy.

"Hey, relax." He laughed. "And clean up your language. You know I can't hear you, but I can imagine what you're saying. And it's not very lady-like, now, is it? Please try to calm down. I've got my own choice words to say to you, too."

A group of kids piled out of Friendly's and gave him strange looks. Embarrassed, Alvin pretended he was blowing his nose and not really holding a conversation with a knotted handkerchief. When they got into a car and roared away, he let out a sigh.

"I'm just lucky I haven't been picked up by the police for loitering or lunacy or other insane acts. With you around, it's hard to stay out of trouble. Now, are you going to be decent and mature about this and let me have my say? Or am I going to have to tie this handkerchief around a parking meter and then take a nice long stroll?"

The handkerchief twitched with increasing fury.

Alvin laughed. "I take it that's a yes?"

He peered into the handkerchief again. Cupid Delaney's feelers were going crazy, rotating around her head like hyperactive windmills.

"Hey, are you all right?"

Alarm flared in him as the beady eyes turned baleful, the wings drooped. He untied the knots hurriedly.

75

"If that Dawn hurt you, I'll . . . hey!"

With a surge of power, the little butterfly soared out of her prison. Cupid Delaney was free! She exulted in the feel of the wind and in her correct reading of Alvin. She just knew the sensitive boy would fall for the old faltering-feeler routine. Now she darted playfully around his body while he swiped at empty air.

"Not fair!" he growled, trying to catch her. "I saved your life, didn't I? Doesn't that count for anything?"

He was right. Cupid Delaney stopped her teasing midflight and darted behind a car. Seconds later she reappeared in body form, her dancing eyes properly subdued.

"This better?" she murmured.

Alvin threw up his hands and made a face. "Sure, if you meant it. How long's the downcast little nun act going to last? A minute? Ten? Oh, it's no use trying to be serious with you. It really isn't. Something's bothering me, and you'll just bounce those yellow cherub curls around and sparkle the way you do and say you care, but two seconds later you'll be off and laughing again, or worse! Plotting how to steal our hearts away from us."

Cupid Delaney began to smile—he was so darn cute when he was serious!—but then managed to keep a straight face. Something really was bothering Alvin. She could tell now by the slump of his shoulders and the flatness of his voice. His warm brown eyes behind the horn rims seemed tired. He looked beaten.

"All right," she said in what she hoped was an encouraging manner. "What is it?"

But she had a feeling she knew. Her little brainstorm about nominating Helen for the Spirit Club had worked. Hadn't Dawn and her cronies just said as much? So Helen had probably told Alvin the news. Alvin was no dummy. He could put two and two together. He had witnessed Craig's romantic attack on Helen, had seen her run away. But if she were to join the Spirit Club, wouldn't that put her in direct and all-too-frequent contact with Craig? And although Alvin was completely sure of his feelings for Helen, was he as sure of Helen's for him? Especially since the girl had seemed so radiant about the invitation. But what was probably galling Alvin, what was sticking in his throat right now, Cupid Delaney realized, was that . . .

"She accepted!" Alvin cried, shaking his head so vigorously his glasses slid down his nose. "I can't believe she accepted. And what's worse is that she seems to think these people, these phony, plastic people, are gods. I can't understand it. That coming from Helen. Sweet, unaffected, down-to-earth Helen."

Cupid Delaney cleared her throat and made appropriate soothing noises. Alvin stared at her suspiciously but continued.

"You know what really gets me? I had something really special to show Helen today. It's something I made, for an exhibit. And I was just asking her to come see it when she looks at me like I'm not even there and goes, 'Oh, Alvin, I can't. I've got to go shopping to get a new outfit for the meeting tomorrow.' And then she pats my arm, like I'm a pet or something, and says, 'You understand, don't you?' and rushes off. Do I understand?" He raised his eyes to Cupid. "No, I *don't* understand. Everything's messed up since yesterday. Craig coming on to Helen. Then her invitation to join this snooty club. I don't know where I stand anymore."

Poor Alvin, Cupid Delaney thought. He doesn't realize how much Helen yearns to look and be like the popular kids. She wasn't happy being herself, not the way Alvin seemed to be.

What was making him unhappy, however, was having his dream girl turn out to be a stranger. She sighed. If only there was a way to ease into the revelations with Helen. Ways that wouldn't hurt so much. She didn't like to watch her subjects suffer—

Hey, wait a minute. Back up there, Cupid, old girl. Remember the *Cupid Handbook*: "A cupid must be objective toward her subjects." Was she feeling objective about Alvin? Or something else? She eyed the springy red hair, the dejected slump of the shoulders, and then heard herself say, "Take me. To the exhibit, I mean. I'd like to see it."

Alvin glanced over, startled.

"Really. I would like to see something you made." Already the idea was taking on the delightful overtones of an adventure. Cupid Delaney hopped impatiently from one white-booted foot to the other.

Alvin gnawed at his lower lip. On the one hand, he was furious with this wretched little cherub. Furious for blowing into his town, his school, his love life. You started out all angry, knowing you were right, and the next thing you knew, she was gazing at you with those incredible blue green eyes, making you feel important and special, like you were ten feet tall, and how could you stay angry with such an attractive and unusual girl?

He hesitated, debating with himself. "You sure you're not just saying that, about wanting to see the exhibit?"

"I was never more serious in my life."

She smiled at him, then reached out and tweaked his scarf. Alvin unthawed.

"OK, you're on. But how do we get there: drive or fly?" They laughed together. It was a start.

Twenty minutes later Alvin motioned Cupid into an old warehouse at the edge of town.

"I don't get it," Cupid Delaney said. "A warehouse?"

A ticket collector at the cavernous door stopped him, but Alvin said, "Danziger, A. I've got an exhibit. Track 47."

The collector, an elderly man wearing a train engineer's cap, checked out a clipboard, then chuckled. "It's a beauty, at that. Go right in."

Now Cupid Delaney was really mystified. "*Track* 47?"

She looked around. Her mouth fell open. The interior of the warehouse resembled a little boy's dream come true. There were trains—all shapes, all models, all sizes—displayed on tracks laid out on the floor. There were realistic backdrops and settings, winter scenes with phony snow and a mirror lake and toy people sledding down a Styrofoam hill and stretches of desert and mountains and ocean. Animated enthusiasts and builders clustered at the exhibits. In the background came the sound of a steam locomotive, pulsing and thundering.

Cupid Delaney looked around and shook her head. "It can't be!"

Alvin grinned. "It isn't. It's just a recording. For atmosphere, I guess. None of the main exhibits, like the granddaddy full-size engines in the corner, are working. They're on tracks, but they're just for show. Some of the models work, though. Come on."

"Only if we get to see yours."

"You're on."

79

He led her halfway across the warehouse, stopping to point out other displays or to greet other hobbyists. Finally he halted in front of track 47. A complete miniature railroad line, looking grimy and used and totally real, rested against the weirdest backdrop Cupid Delaney had ever seen. Alvin had not been content to resurrect the usual New England setting with town square and church steeple and small pond. He had gone thirty steps further and created a new world, one that looked like it belonged in the twenty-first century. The houses were glass dwellings, the people wore space suits, and the tracks were raised high above the ground. It was very original and had drawn many admirers.

Alvin peered at Cupid Delaney nervously.

"You like it?"

She shook her head slowly. "No."

His face fell and she added, "I *love* it. It's tremendous."

"Oh." A big grin appeared.

A small boy popped up between them. "Hey, mister, you make this?"

Alvin nodded.

"Can you make it go? I want to see it go round that pointy tower and then across that crazy bridge."

"Well, um, I've got a minor problem with the tracks up there," Alvin said. He looked apologetically around him. The crowd muttered.

Cupid Delaney had an idea. "I think I want to take a ride."

"What!"

She ignored his horrified look.

"Don't worry. It'll be fun! More fun than flying."

"Now, hold on a minute. Don't do anything crazy," Alvin said. But it was too late. The wretched creature did what she wanted anyway. Unlike a certain other sweet girl he knew. Oh, how he regretted inviting Cupid Delaney to the model train show. Why couldn't it have been Helen by his side? Because Helen was off buying clothes for a Spirit Club meeting, he thought bitterly. And all because of this—this emissary from the Love Bureau.

He turned to give Cupid Delaney a piece of his mind, but she was gone. And the next instant the red light glowed on his control box. Someone—some*thing*—had switched it on.

"All right!" the little boy cried as the tiny train and attached cars began to rumble into life. The eight-piece unit took off slowly, but as it went down an incline, picked up speed. Was it louder, more realistic-sounding than the other trains in the show, or was that his imagination? Alvin bit his lip and frowned. It had never sounded so lifelike before. Other people from neighboring exhibits began to press closer. And then, as the fiercely puffing locomotive roared around the track, Alvin spotted a tiny butterfly feeler just inside the window.

"Oh, no," he breathed. He fiddled with the controls, but it was no use. Cupid Delaney had taken over and was playing chief engineer.

"Daddy, come look at this!" The little boy pulled at his father's hand. "The train's going to go up and around that tower!"

The crowd moved in closer. "It'll never make it," someone said. "The curve's too steep."

"You wanna make a bet?" the boy crowed. "Watch!"

Alvin held his breath as the thundering train zoomed around the track and up the incline to the tower. "Cupid, Cupid," he mumbled, half in admiration and half in fear. What was she going to do? Push his train beyond its limits? Create the biggest crash of the afternoon?

That was what the crowd thought. They were craning their necks to get a better view, predicting when the train would fly off course. If he reckoned right, it would be just at the sharpest curve above the tower, right before the bridge. The bridge! He looked over and saw that it was closed. Alvin tried to push the switch to divert the train. Nothing happened.

"Cupid Delaney, jump ship!" he cried. Of course, she couldn't hear him. The roar of the engine and now the train's piercing wail obliterated all sound. Did he imagine it, or could he detect her laughing as she rolled by again? Oh, it was crazy. And there was no stopping her now as the locomotive branched off to head for the tower.

"There she goes," said the boy.

"There she goes," echoed Alvin, clutching his forehead. Everyone held his breath as the train ate up the tracks, gathered a rush of speed, and then, hesitating at the deadman's curve like a roller coaster, plunged screechingly around the curve—and flew off into space.

"Oh, no!" Alvin cried, but then was struck dumb as the train soared gracefully *over* the bridge and landed with cat-footed sureness on the tracks below. Hooting gaily several times, it clung to the path and finally rumbled to a stop in front of the control box and a shaking Alvin. The crowd went wild. People cheered and clapped Alvin on the back.

"Oh, boy!" The little boy's eyes sparkled. "Oh, boy!"

A man came up and shook Alvin's hand. "If you aren't accepted in the Essex County Model Engineers Society, I'll eat my hat."

Alvin ran a hand self-consciously through his hair and glowed. He felt a tap on his shoulder and turned. Cupid Delaney stood there, her eyes dancing, her golden hair windblown.

"Wow!" she whispered. "That was great! That train of yours beats flying by wing anytime."

Alvin grabbed the girl's hands and whirled her around in an exhilarating little dance.

"What's all this about?" She was giggling, trying not to step on his toes.

"I might make the Model Engineers Society! That's a dream of a lifetime! Oh, you're wonderful, you know that? Thank you!"

As he dipped and twirled her, Cupid Delaney pulled slightly away.

"Well, if you really feel that way," she said, arching a mischievous eyebrow, "could I go back and do it again?"

Alvin threw back his head and laughed. And Cupid Delaney, joining in, felt like the sleeping princess in the fairy tale who is awakened by a kiss: scared, alive, and very enchanted by the prince.

The Nerdette Succumbs

Wednesday morning dawned bright and clear, a pleasant change from the cold rain of the night before. The sun peeked out from behind fluffy clouds, promising warmer temperatures and perfect conditions for the upcoming school championship game.

Underneath her blanket of leaves, Cupid Delaney yawned and stretched. Carefully, oh, so slowly, a feeler poked out, followed by her head and then her wings. She scanned the park. No one was in sight, except a few noisy squirrels and a small black dog who sniffed deliberately around the jungle gym. All clear. Cupid Delaney surveyed her far-from-deluxe single-room accommodations and smiled. Two days ago she would have grumbled like mad to have to sleep in the park, but two days ago she hadn't gone with Alvin to the exhibit and had so much fun. Two days ago she had only known Alvin as a carefully researched subject, and now they were friends. Just friends? she asked herself, staring up at the sky and feeling as light and buoyant as the clouds.

Just friends, Valentina would respond quickly and firmly. *And not even that. A cupid must never, ever become entangled in any way with her subjects.*

Not even a cute/ugly, wonderfully brilliant, and often hilarious one?

Not even then. Especially not then. You know the rules.

Yes, Cupid Delaney sighed. I know the rules. But I always did have trouble keeping them. And yesterday had been so much fun. For once she had gotten to be the one to go out with a boy and not fix someone else up. For once she had gotten to be the bride and not the perennial bridesmaid. Oh, sure, seeing a train exhibit was not exactly the stuff of which dreams are made, but being with Alvin, laughing, talking, and dancing in that one brief, crazy moment had meant more to her than all the romantic matches she had forged.

Whoa, slow down there. How could she have said that, *meant* that? She took little hopping leaps in her agitation. How could she dream of flying up and becoming a certified cupid if one simple episode with a boy turned her mind inside out? Because it's not my mind, she thought. She landed on a pile of leaves and, frowning, scuffled out of it.

I'm in trouble, she thought. A person on Weight Watchers who stops by a pastry shop and hungers after the big, gooey chocolate eclair in the window. My nose is up to the glass, and I want in. I want the same things every red-blooded high school girl wants from a romance: buying a dress for a special date, receiving candy or flowers from an admirer, anticipating the big dance. I want to flirt and laugh and hold hands with a boy. I want to enjoy a first kiss. I want Alvin, her heart whispered.

Forget it, Valentina's voice suddenly rumbled in her mind. *Temptation comes to us all, but we fight it. Because we're more than mortal, if somewhat less than the gods. To give in to personal romance would be to forfeit this mission and every other mission thereafter. To say good-bye to cupid wings and romantic power and magic spells. To say hello to scribbling greeting-card verses or working at a video dating agency or any number of the mundane jobs fallen cupids usually take. Is that what you want? Is that what you've been trained for?*

No! Cupid Delaney cried. No. It's just that I—that Alvin—oh, never mind. You're right. Even if we did have fun yesterday at the show, it was just that and nothing more to Alvin. I was just a stand-in. His heart belongs to Helen. A real live girl. Not a reasonable facsimile of one.

Now you're talking some sense, the Sweetheart Squad leader's voice said. *I knew you'd see the light. But, Delaney? Get going on this project. The dance is the day after tomorrow.*

As if I'd ever forget, Cupid Delaney thought. However, she was guilty of goofing off yesterday afternoon, playing steam locomotive engineer when she should have been finding out what the girls in the Spirit Club were up to. Something sneaky was going on. She knew that from the conversation at Friendly's. Just before Dawn had gone crazy and tried to impale her on a straw. And she was supposed to match this—this teenage barbarian with a sweet and sensitive boy like Alvin? It didn't make sense. The couples didn't make sense. The original pairs were the right ones, Cupid Delaney thought. Helen and Alvin on one hand, and Dawn and Craig on the other. Mixing and matching them like so many dishes of Chinese food did not seem right.

Still, the Love Bureau had an impressive success ratio, with ninety-nine and seven-eighths percent of all couples working out and dating happily ever after. Their colossally expensive computer was state-of-the-art. Valentina might be irritable and self-centered, but her nose for romance was renowned throughout all the major divisions. And that nose had told her that Helen and Craig and Dawn and Alvin were compatible.

Well, Cupid Delaney sniffed, so be it. If that's what Valentina wants, that's what Valentina will get. She looked up at the sun. It was rising in the sky. It must be close to seven o'clock, she estimated. Time to pay little unobtrusive social calls on her subjects on this very important morning, the day of the big homecoming rally, followed by the Spirit Club meeting at Dawn's.

First stop: the hunkette's bedroom, where she'd try to figure out what the evil trio was plotting against Helen. Mustn't let a human trick her at her own game!

Dawn had already finished painting the fingernails of both hands a bright red by the time Cupid Delaney gained entry to the house and to her bedroom. The cheerleader was sitting in front of her vanity, dressed in a short pink satin robe, alternately blowing on her wet polish and setting up her hot rollers. There was a manic quality about all her movements, as if someone had pushed her button to fast forward, but her violet eyes glittered and she was humming along to the heavy-metal rock that pulsated from her radio. Her energy wasn't motivated by fear or desperation, Cupid Delaney realized, but anticipation.

But anticipation of what?

The phone rang on the dresser. Dawn hurriedly jabbed a hot roller in her hair and then leaned across to answer it.

"Hello. . . . Oh, hi, Craig!" Her momentarily irritated tone altered dramatically. Cupid Delaney twitched at the sound of his name. What in the world was he doing calling Dawn? The little butterfly edged out slightly from behind the roller case, keeping her wings tucked in.

Dawn was sticking the rollers in her hair as she cradled the phone. "What? No, I *told* you, everything's set for the party later. All the kids know Helen's coming. . . . Well, of course I told them! I wouldn't just spring it on them. . . ." Cupid heard a male voice babbling as Dawn made a face and muttered something rude. The girl gritted her teeth and returned to the conversation. "For pity's sake, we're not antisocial clods, Craig! Naturally we're going to be friendly to Helen. Yes, *very* friendly. Don't worry." Her voice softened. "Now remember what you promised? That we'd talk about the Grid if I invited Helen to my party. . . . All right, *after* the party if you insist, but I don't see why we can't discuss it now. . . . What? Oh, I see." The red claws tightened on the phone, but she managed a light laugh. "You have to go pick up Helen this morning and see if she's all right. I see. Well, don't let me keep you from your mission. . . . Yes, all right. See you later, good-bye."

The phone crashed down so hard several hot rollers fell from her hair. Cupid Delaney took one look at the girl's face and retreated behind the case. Dawn was in such a vicious mood that the butterfly feared for her life if she were discovered. She had to get out of there, fast. But, inching her way to the slightly open bedroom window, she heard Dawn laugh.

Turning, she saw the dark-haired girl grinning at the mirror.

"Are we going to be friendly to Helen?" she asked. "Oh, yes, Craig, never fear. We're going to be *very* friendly to the dear little mouse." She threw back her head and laughed.

Cupid Delaney left the girl's bedroom, puzzling over her remarks. Something was going to happen to Helen at the party tonight, but she didn't know what. The butterfly shivered and turned in the direction of the intended victim's house.

At 7:24 the Mapeses were gathered in the living room. They were discussing Helen's new outfit, while the girl stood there self-consciously.

Chloris Mapes clucked disapprovingly. "I don't know, I really don't know. That skirt seems so short."

"It's supposed to be that length," Dorothy said. "That's what all the magazines show."

"And that sweater vest. It's, well, a little loud, isn't it? That bright pink. And perhaps a bit too snug?"

"Oh, Mother," Helen said. She glanced impatiently at her watch.

"I think it's great!" Ethel said in a wistful voice. "I wish I could wear an outfit like that."

"Well, you're too young. Thank goodness for that."

"I don't know, Chlo." Harold Mapes smiled nervously. "I think our girl looks nice. Pretty and different."

"Oh, Daddy, you're terrific." Helen ran over and hugged him. She pulled away and looked at her mother with pleading eyes.

Mrs. Mapes frowned. "I don't know. I really don't know."

"Please, Mommy?" Now Ethel and Dorothy got in the act.

She smiled grudgingly. "I take it I'm outvoted. All right. Go ahead and wear it today, and I hope it makes you a hit at this Spirit event or whatever it is you've been talking about."

"Oh, Mom, thanks!" Helen leaned over and pecked her cheek. "I've got to dash. I told Alvin I'd ride with him this morning, and he's always so punctual. I'll just grab my coat and—"

The doorbell rang, startling Cupid Delaney more than anyone else. She was perched just inside the rim of the umbrella stand, and the piercing ring made her lose her balance and tumble backwards. Luckily, Mr. Mapes' galoshes cushioned her fall, and she got back on her feet gingerly. Honestly, she grumbled, the Love Bureau should have special insurance coverage for their agents.

"I'll get it," Helen said, going to the door. "It's probably Alvin, and—oh. Oh, it's *you!*"

Craig's movie-star features and muscular frame appeared in the doorway. Helen stepped back, completely flustered. Her family let out a collective admiring gasp. For a few seconds, no one spoke. Then all at once, Mrs. Mapes made birdlike cries, "Where are my manners? Come in, come in"; Ethel and Dorothy burst out giggling; and Craig, beaming idiotically at his beloved, said, "Hi, Helen. Can I take you to school?"

"School?" Helen stared at Craig with dreamy eyes.

Dorothy nudged her sister. "Yeah, you know, that place called Woodside you've been going to for three years now."

While Helen remained speechless, returning Craig's intense stare, Mrs. Mapes cooed, "Go on, Helen! Go. You just said you didn't want to be late. And this nice young man is offering to take you. Oh, by the way, I'm Chloris Mapes, Helen's mother." She offered a trembling hand. Craig took it, still gazing at Helen. "And this is my husband, Harold." Again the absentee handshake. "And my other two girls, Dorothy and Ethel."

"Hi!" Two pairs of awestruck eyes devoured Craig, but his gaze merely flicked over them before returning to Helen.

"Helen? Go along now, it's getting late." Mrs. Mapes went to the closet and pulled out her daughter's coat. "Here, put this on." Like a doll, Helen allowed herself to be dressed.

"Now, go!" Mrs. Mapes gave her a gentle push. Helen moved like a sleepwalker to the front door where Craig waited, the groom watching his bride come down the aisle. When she reached him, he held out his hand. Helen hesitated. The whole family leaned forward and held its breath. With a little sigh, Helen placed her hand in his.

"Oh, Harold," Mrs. Mapes whispered, dabbing at her eyes with her apron. "This is so romantic."

Mr. Mapes cleared his throat and patted his wife's shoulder. Together they watched the most handsome and popular senior at Woodside escort their daughter to his car. With infinite care, he settled her inside, then slid into the driver's seat and started the motor.

And what about Alvin Danziger? Cupid Delaney felt like asking the Mapes family. You remember Alvin, the thin, red-haired kid with horn rims and an unforgettable smile? The boy who was so good to your daughter before the hunk Craig entered the picture? Will Alvin be casually tossed out for this impressive and dazzling new model?

As if on cue, Alvin drove into view and parked his VW right behind the silver Fiat just as Craig gunned his motor and pulled away.

Alvin peered after the car and jumped out.

"Hey!" he cried. "Helen?"

He turned to the house, where Mr. and Mrs. Mapes exchanged sheepish glances.

"What happened?" Alvin demanded, standing feet squarely apart, hands on hips. He sounded angry, but Cupid Delaney heard the disappointment in his voice.

"Did He-Man Lacrosse barge right in and sweep Helen away? I should have known. I should have gotten here sooner." He pounded a fist against his leg.

Ethel and Dorothy broke out giggling. Mr. Mapes shooed them into the kitchen, leaving Chloris Mapes to face the music. But Alvin had said his piece. The person he really had to talk to was being whisked away in the prince's royal silver carriage.

"Such a lovely boy," Chloris Mapes said, smiling brightly. "That Craig."

"Yes, lovely," Alvin echoed. There was a dangerous grin on his face.

Cupid Delaney rolled her beady black eyes. If she wanted to prevent a murder, she had to distract Alvin's attention. Edging her way out of the galoshes, she took off through the door and made straight for Alvin's face. Seeing the brightly colored wings, the boy backed up.

"You!" he hissed under his breath. "I should have known. Get lost."

He strode back to the car and slammed the door, ignoring the frantic motions of the tiny butterfly by the windshield. Cupid Delaney flapped her wings, until he took pity and rolled down the window. Quickly, she breathed a question into his ear.

"What's wrong?" Alvin gave her a cold stare from behind the wheel. "As if you didn't know. Bringing Craig here this morning to take Helen to school. Getting those cheerleaders to invite her to join the Spirit Club. All nicely arranged by a certain

92

little cupid, wasn't it? Everything all arranged and I mean everything. Even the offer to come see the trains yesterday afternoon? I thought that was spontaneous and also very special. But it really was listed on the Love Bureau menu!"

He turned away from her agitated dance and started the car. Cupid gave up the battle and stopped her useless flapping. The beat-up VW roared off down the street, Alvin hunched angrily at the wheel.

Inside the open doorway, Mrs. Mapes shook her head. "What a strange boy." The door closed slowly behind her.

Alvin Crashes a Party

Alvin showed up at Dawn's house at five o'clock, determined to play Saint George to the Spirit Club dragon should Helen need him. Dawn opened the door to his insistent ring.

"You!" she gasped, staring at him on her doorstep. "What are you doing here?"

Alvin gave her a tight smile. "Collecting for the Send the Loch Ness Monster to College Fund. Helen asked me to this Spirit Club meeting. Now, may I come in? Or do I have to call your mother and tell her you're being rude to one of your invited guests?"

Good manners warred with irritation and won. Dawn shrugged and ungraciously motioned Alvin inside.

"Thank you for your very charming and warm welcome," he said. "It's nice to know there's so much more to your personality than you ever reveal. Has the meeting gotten started or are the tribal initiation rites still going on?"

Their eyes battled for a moment. Then Dawn turned on her heel and walked back to the den. Alvin laughed softly and shut the front door. "Don't want any conniving little butterflies slipping in," he muttered and followed the girl.

But it was too late. Cupid Delaney had reconnoitered earlier that afternoon and had gained entry to the Cummingses' house through the laundry-room window. For the past hour she had been hiding behind one of the massive stereo speakers in the den. From this position she had a perfect ringside seat for the upcoming fireworks of the Spirit Club meeting, but her hearing was slowly being eroded. One more Stones album and she'd have to risk moving to another hiding place.

Alvin came into the crowded room and her heart leaped. So much for objectivity toward subjects, she thought. She couldn't do anything about it, but she realized she had feelings for this reedy carrot top. It had never happened to her before, and it would probably never happen to her again, but she knew she had been zapped. Just as she had zapped thousands of subjects. Look at how depressed she had been all afternoon remembering the angry parting with Alvin at the Mapeses' house.

The little butterfly watched Alvin scan the room for Helen, his eyes lighting up when he spotted her. If only he would realize he was wasting his time on this girl. If only he could discover that her true self was 180 degrees different from the shy, plain image she projected. Alvin Danziger was infatuated with the wrong girl and that was all there was to it.

And so who's the right girl? Valentina's voice whispered in her ear. *You? You're not even a girl; you're a would-be cupid, so don't get any funny ideas. Just stick to the mission and the mission will reward you with wings. But you've got to complete the mission.*

All right, all right, I heard you, Sweetheart Squad leader. I'll focus on my subjects just as subjects. No more fantasizing—and certainly not on company time. The little black eyes swept the room. Concentrate, she ordered herself. This meet-

95

ing could make or break Helen's relationship with Craig. Her eyes settled on the quiet girl who was busy talking to both Craig and Alvin at the same time.

She wasn't the only one observing Helen. Cupid Delaney noted that out of the eleven kids present, at least four others—all the girls of the club—were doing likewise. She didn't like that. There was something a little disturbing in the way these four girls fixated on Helen. Dawn, Wendy, Claire, and Beth Simpson, the senior class secretary, huddled in a corner and cackled together like witches. There were smug grins on their faces and an air of impatience in the way they'd devour Helen with their eyes and then glance at their watches. Just like cannibals might look if invited to a missionary meeting.

She wanted to circulate and discover the reason for their animation but was afraid to move from her hiding place. If Alvin realized she was eavesdropping, it would be all over. She had to play it safe, as much as that went against her usual impulsive methods.

Luck was on her side. Tom Delacruz came up and said something to Dawn. The girl looked at her watch, then eyed her friends and nodded. She motioned for Ted Abatto, the outgoing yearbook editor, to kill the music, and silence finally descended on the gathering.

At last, Cupid Delaney thought. My poor ears.

Dawn straightened her shoulders, adjusted the neckline of her daring lace blouse, and walked to the center of the room. She held up a perfectly manicured hand. Some of the kids who were laughing by the refreshment table sheepishly subsided and came to sit on the two sofas that faced each other by the fireplace. Craig continued to whisper to Helen.

Alvin sat next to them, his face a stony mask, his dejection evident for all to see.

The cheerleader pointedly cleared her throat and glared at the offending couple. Finally Alvin nudged Craig, and he and Helen reluctantly broke apart.

"Now, do I have everyone's attention?" Dawn asked. "This is a very special Spirit Club meeting. And I say special for a very good reason. Today we have a guest with us, well, actually, two guests. You've met them, I'm sure, but let me take a moment for proper introductions. Helen Mapes, could you stand up?" She gestured toward the sofa, and Helen quickly withdrew her hand from Craig's and got nervously to her feet. Her face was bright red. "All right, you can sit down, Helen." Dawn laughed softly, but Cupid Delaney could detect the hostility behind the friendliness. "And with her is a *special guest*"—she emphasized the two words for Craig's benefit—"Alvin Danziger. Alvin?"

The red-haired boy gave an unenthusiastic nod and slumped back in his seat. Poor Alvin, Cupid Delaney thought. He was having a rough day. Her heart went out to him. First Helen going out of her way to avoid him at school and now all but ignoring him at the party.

Dawn produced a pad and pen. "OK," she announced, "the reason we're here. As you're all well aware, the big game is tomorrow, and since we know Woodside's going to win—"

"What do you mean, win?" Tom broke in. "More like slaughter poor West Orange! Decimate them! Trounce 'em, bounce 'em, jounce 'em into the ground!"

Cheers and more claps rang out until Dawn laughed and held up a restraining hand. "As Spirit Club organizers, it's our job to make other kids' enthusiasm as charged up as Tom's. Now you all know we do the usual things before our games—the rallies, the cheers, the interclass rivalries. And traditionally, the night before the homecoming game, we honor the players."

Tom's quick grin flashed again. "You call toilet-papering our front lawns an honor? My dad calls it something else. How about yours, Craig?"

But Craig was not listening. He was intently scribbling notes to an embarrassed Helen, who'd read them with a shy smile before shaking her head. Alvin glowered in his seat, a volcano poised for eruption.

Dawn tapped the pen on the pad, like a judge bringing order to an unruly courtroom. "If I could have everyone's attention, especially our guests'?" she asked smartly. Helen bit her lip and pushed aside Craig's latest communication. She leaned forward as if to demonstrate her undivided attention.

"Thank you, Helen. You see, you're an integral part of this evening's meeting. When Craig first brought up your name, I admit I was a little hesitant. I mean, I didn't really know anything about you, but I see now it was a great idea. Because you're the only one who can help carry off our new homecoming project. It's a fantastic idea, one that Claire thought up, and very daring. And since you're interested in joining our organization . . . ?"

Helen nodded eagerly.

"This little project will serve in place of other qualifications or requirements. If you agree to work on the plan, then you'll automatically be considered for membership. And if you go one step further and carry out the plan, why, then there's no question. You're in. Immediately. Full member, all the rights and privileges. What do you say, are you interested so far?"

"A trap," Cupid Delaney whispered, her mind racing. "It's a trap. Don't fall for it, Helen. Realize you're in way over your head and leave."

But the quiet girl was fidgeting on the sofa in barely concealed excitement. There was no way Ms. Invisible was going to turn down a chance of a lifetime: the invitation to be accepted into the most popular club at school. What did she have to do: white out all the spots on an untamed leopard? Give an eel a rubber ducky and a bath? Fail all her courses for the rest of the year? It didn't matter. She'd do it. And gladly. Anything, finally, to exchange the Nobody name tag at Woodside for the Somebody. This was her chance. Alone she couldn't do it. But with Craig by her side, she could do anything. Leap from nerdette to Somebody status in less than a week. Already several boys in her classes were giving her the eye after seeing Craig paying her court. Think of how much more assured her position would be if she made the Spirit Club. Half the girls at school yearned for that honor. And she, Helen Mapes, formerly a nonentity, would have it.

She squeezed Craig's hand and gave him a radiant smile. "Count me in," she announced to one and all in the voice of a street urchin joining a band of cutthroat pirates. Dawn purred with happiness. The girls in the room eyed one another and winked. Alvin swung his head and stared at his beloved's hand intertwined with Craig's. Then he looked up and frowned at Dawn.

"Would someone like to tell me," he said softly, "what is going on?"

Hear! Hear! Cupid Delaney thought. I second that emotion.

Dawn looked flustered for a moment but regained her poise. "We're having a Spirit Club meeting," she said icily. "We're asking Helen to help

99

us with a new project. We think she'll be perfect for it."

"Why? What is it?"

She held herself straighter, pursed her lips. "I don't think that's any of your business. This is supposed to be a closed, private meeting, and I allowed you in only because Helen invited you."

"I did *what*?" Helen looked at Alvin in surprise. Alvin raised his hands in mute apology, then shrugged.

"So I got in under false pretenses. What are you going to do: cut off my tongue to swear me to secrecy? I won't go around babbling your club's plans to the kids at school, and I'm certainly not a spy for West Orange. I merely asked how Helen fitted in with this exciting and daring new project you've been talking about. I'm curious."

You're not the only one, Cupid Delaney thought. Come on, Dawn, give. Don't clam up now.

Dawn hesitated. "If the rest of the members don't mind?"

No one did. She was forced to continue and she did, gazing sourly at Alvin from time to time. Briefly she described the intense but friendly football rivalry between the West Orange and Woodside high schools. She talked about the various pranks each school had played on the other until the practice had been banned by both principals involved.

"It's been nearly three years, and West Orange is not expecting anything funny from us," she went on. "That's why when Helen pulls off this stunt, they'll be caught off guard. It'll be fantastic."

The members of the Spirit Club had been briefed earlier by phone and now smiled at one another knowingly. Craig touched Helen's sleeve. "I know you can do it," he whispered.

Alvin blew out an exasperated breath. "Do *what,* for heaven's sake! What's Helen going to do?"

"Why, steal West Orange's mascot," Dawn said, grinning. "That six-foot, moldy excuse for an eagle."

A Cupid in Trouble

The Sweetheart Squad leaders were bored. They had been up all night planning Valentine's Day activities for the Northeastern division and now sat slumped over the computer consoles, barely stifling yawns.

"What time is it?" Enchantée asked in a lazy voice, one finger idly twisting her silken blonde curls.

Bella Rosa leaned her exotically dark head out the window to gaze at the courtyard below. "Don't know," she murmured. "The sundial's hidden from here. It must be at least ten, though."

"Ten. In the morning?"

Passionata giggled and nodded.

Enchantée's brow puckered. "What do we do until noon? We don't have anything scheduled."

Bella Rosa slid in next to Enchantée at the console and rapidly punched the keys. Mystified, the others watched as the video screen over their heads flickered into life and two animated, gesticulating teenagers sprang into view.

"What's this?" Passionata asked. "A 'Leave It to Beaver' rerun?"

"This, my dear friends, is the true-to-life drama of one of our most dangerous yet endearing cupid trainees. This is the mission of . . ." She paused dramatically and they all giggled and chimed in, "Cupid Delaney!"

"Bring it into focus and get the pertinent data of the subjects on the screen so we can follow the plot so far."

The video camera zoomed in on Dawn and Craig. They were arguing outside the school cafeteria. Actually, Dawn was performing a monologue while Craig towered calmly over her. When her speech became more animated, the Senior Sweetheart leaders leaned forward.

"Turn it up," Enchantée urged, no longer bored. "I don't want to miss a word. Oh, this is better than 'All My Cherubs.'"

Bella Rosa adjusted the sound and Dawn's injured tones clearly filled the hallway. The leaders shook their heads.

". . . What do you mean, asked Helen to the Grid?" she said. "You told me you were going to ask me if I invited her to the Spirit Club meeting. Well, I did invite her, and more than that, she's practically a full-blown member if she pulls off this stunt today. So I don't get it."

"I said I wanted to talk to you about the Grid. That didn't mean inviting you."

As if she had been slapped, Dawn's face flushed. But she managed a forced laugh. "What *did* it mean then?"

Craig shook his head slowly, an embarrassed frown on his face. "I'm sorry, Dawn, I wanted to ask you to help Helen pick something out for the dance. You know, a really spectacular dress. I know how much she admires you, and she'd love it."

"That's just peachy," Dawn quavered, "but would *I*?"

Realizing the awkwardness of the situation, Craig swallowed and took a step back. "Look, I'm sorry, Dawn. I really am. But you have to know that Helen Mapes is the only girl for me. I'm crazy about her. You must have thousands of guys who'd jump to take you to the dance."

"I've turned down all the other guys," she said coolly. "Everyone has a date by now."

"Everyone?" Craig asked innocently. "What about Alvin Danziger?"

A low, insensitive blow. Dawn's eyes blazed.

"Alvin Danziger? He happens to be one of the last boys in the school I'd go to the Grid with. As if you didn't know. But you don't know. You're so—infatuated with this Helen person, I swear you're on a different planet these days. You and Helen both. The Planet of the Mapes." She brushed past Craig, head held high, then stopped and looked back, disdain in her eyes. "Don't worry about me and the Grid. I'm sure I'll be able to muster up a date or two. This girl knows there's plenty of fish in the sea."

And with an angry swish of her long hair, she walked off.

"Oh, dear." Bella Rosa sighed, raising her eyebrows. "Cupid Delaney's in trouble. The printout states that Helen is Craig's choice for the dance and Dawn is Alvin's. Did you hear what Dawn said about Alvin? There's no way those two can be romantically reconciled at this late date. Our little cupid trainee's in big trouble."

"And we don't even know if Helen agreed to be Craig's date," said Enchantée. "Cupid Delaney might not even accomplish half her mission."

The three Senior Sweetheart leaders looked at one another in alarm.

"See if you can locate her, quick!"

Bella Rosa fumbled with the console, the huge video screen fast-forwarding scenes of Woodside High activities. "Come out," she mumbled, "come out, come out, wherever you are. Ah. There! In disguise."

104

The screen focused on a chemistry lab, more specifically, on the tiny fluttering of a butterfly wing behind a bunsen burner.

"Is she crazy?" Enchantée exclaimed. "That thing could go off any minute, and she'd be gone in a second."

They clucked together with motherly concern and stared at the screen. To the right of the bunsen burner stood a very tense Alvin. Across the black lab counter stood an equally tense Helen.

"More problems in Adolescent City?" murmured Passionata. She threw up her hands. "This mission's on a very rocky course."

"You mean little Delaney is. Wait until Valentina finds out." Bella Rosa frowned and adjusted the audio control. Alvin's bewildered voice was heard clearly, even though he was whispering.

"You can't be serious about this afternoon, Helen. You know it's crazy and not going to work."

Helen glanced over her shoulder at Mrs. Gallagher before replying.

"Don't be so negative, Alvin. You're always so pessimistic. I'm going to follow Dawn's instructions, and it can't fail. The West Orange mascot will be ours. And I'll be the one to do it! Isn't that exciting?"

He took one look at her shining eyes and groaned. "Exciting? The only thing exciting I see coming out of all this crazy nonsense is your being caught and suspended from school. Is that exciting to you?"

"I don't care," she retorted, one dark curl escaping from her headband. "It'll be worth it to me. I'll be in the Spirit Club, an official member, and no one can take that away from me."

"The Spirit Club, the Spirit Club, that's all you ever talk about. Can't you hear yourself? Can't you see how you've changed since Monday? You used to be interested in chess and studying together and going with me to the hobby stores, but now it's all shopping at the mall, getting dressed up, talking about makeup and who's wearing what to the dance. Can't you see how you've changed?" Alvin swept aside his microscope and leaned across to take Helen's hand, but she jerked it away in a huff. "All right, don't listen to me," he snapped. "Keep playing palsy-walsy with that two-timing Lothario and his little plastic friends, and you'll end up in trouble. I mean it, Helen. Especially if you listen to the playboy of the playpen set, Craig. He's setting you up. Listen to me. He doesn't really care about you. He—"

"Alvin Danziger!" Mrs. Gallagher's voice cracked like a whip. "Less talk, more work over there."

He nodded automatically, stared down into the lens, but continued to whisper. "I *know* Craig doesn't really care. I have inside information. It's all a big mistake."

Helen's lips trembled, but she faced him defiantly. "That's a lie! Craig asked me to go the Grid with him tomorrow night. Would he ask me if he didn't like me?"

Alvin nodded and leaned across. "That's just it," he said, his eyes flashing, "you don't understand. It's not that Craig wants to go to the dance with you; he just thinks he does. He's been brainwashed. Hypnotized."

Helen straightened up. "I see," she said frostily. "And just who, I ask, might be brainwashing Craig into liking me?"

Alvin hesitated, biting his lip, and she smiled, a cold smile that never reached her eyes.

"You don't believe me," Alvin burst out and then lowered his voice. "You think I'm just saying these things because I'm jealous. OK, I admit I'm a little jealous and it sounds weird, but just listen to me with an open mind. Helen, the person who's been doing all these crazy things to your life and to mine is none other than a cu—cu—cu—" He was stuttering badly, his lips unable to complete the statement.

A tiny butterfly eye popped out from behind the bunsen burner and glared straight at him. He glared back.

"Helen," he said, "there! Behind the bun—bun—bun— The cu—cu—cu— Oh, rats!"

He threw up his hands in disgust and frustration.

"I don't understand your sense of humor lately, Alvin," Helen said reprovingly, "but I can't say that I like it. Now, let's just forget this conversation and concentrate on our lab experiment. Mrs. Gallagher's giving us the evil eye."

"But, Helen," said Alvin feebly, "there really is a cu—cu—cu— Aw, skip it!" He directed a ferocious scowl at the shadow behind the bunsen burner before reapplying himself, not too happily, to the microscope.

"What's all this?" Valentina demanded, sweeping into the computer room. "Having a coffee klatch?"

Bella Rosa hurriedly blanked out the screen, but not before the squad leader glimpsed the depressed face of Alvin.

"Checking out Cupid Delaney's progress? How's it going?"

"Not too—" Passionata began, then felt a pinch on her arm. "Ouch! Er, I mean, outrageously well," she

amended, shooting a murderous look at Enchantée. Enchantée beamed innocently back at her.

Valentina looked smug. "I knew it. Didn't I tell her this mission would be a piece of cake? She'll get her wings for sure on Friday."

"That I very much doubt," Bella Rosa whispered to her friends as the majestic leader swept out. They looked at each other glumly and shook their heads.

Ms. Invisible Takes
Center Stage

At three thirty in the afternoon, a half hour before kickoff at the big game, a nervous butterfly, an exhilarated nerdette, and a glamorous cheerleader were all sitting in a car off West Orange Avenue. Six eyes were glued to the Maple–West Orange intersection. Three hearts were pounding thunderously. One mind kept turning in furious circles and always came back to the same thought: Why did Dawn replace Ted Abatto in the mascot-stealing adventure and what was Dawn secretly smirking about?

Cupid Delaney sidled carefully along the backseat of the racy red Mustang, keeping one eye fixed on Dawn, sitting behind the wheel, and the other on her passenger, Helen. She had to be doubly careful that neither girl spotted her. But she also had to be doubly alert that nothing escaped her observation during this so-called prank. If Helen failed to pull it off, her credit rating would sink to zero among the popular set, she wouldn't make Spirit Club, and Craig might think twice about taking her to the Grid. No, Cupid *had* to keep a firm hand on the controls this afternoon if she wanted to earn her wings and fly up.

Helen turned and looked at Dawn. "You're sure this is the right street and the right place to wait? It's been nearly fifteen minutes."

Dawn smiled. "My information comes from the best sources: Claire's cousin who goes to West Orange used to date the guy who wears the mascot getup. She's out for revenge, and what better timing and opportunity than to help us."

Helen squinted intently at the intersection. "I know, but why are you sure he's going to turn off on West Orange and Maple? It could be any other street, and then we'll miss him and we won't get the chance to get the eagle suit."

"Will you relax? This guy, Pete Grayson, is as regular as clockwork. He goes through the exact same motions at the exact same time before every game. He never deviates for a fraction of a second or a foot. And Claire's cousin should know. She's gone with him to countless games when he plays mascot. So you can just relax that serious little head of yours and start breathing normally again. In just about thirty seconds, Pete will be tootling across Maple and turning onto West Orange Avenue in his parent's blue Camaro. And when he runs out of gas, we'll be positioned perfectly to help him. Now, do you need to run through the instructions again? Or do you have it all down?"

"I've got it all down, but I'm so excited I might forget!"

Dawn witnessed Helen's enthusiasm with concealed distaste and managed a light laugh. "OK, one more time. We want this operation to go smoothly, right?"

Oh, right! Cupid Delaney sniffed sarcastically.

Helen nodded and held up crossed fingers with a giggle. The cheerleader rolled her eyes but held up her own crossed fingers to suggest solidarity and went on. "All right, in twenty seconds or less, because Pete should be on his way. Our man will leave his house on Grosvenor Place at exactly 3:40 and put the eagle suit on the backseat of his car. He'll get in, drive along Grosvenor until he turns on Baker, one right to Maple until he hits West Orange, at which time, bingo! His gas tank will register empty and his car will sputter and die. I got Ted to do the car earlier, so that's all set. Now, he—oops! Hold on." She held up a hand and stared at the intersection. A dark blue Camaro swung slowly into view and stopped at the light.

"Oh, my," Helen said. "Is that him?"

Dawn glanced at her watch and grinned. "Right on the nose. Now listen. We've been through this before, but just remember, let me do all the talking to get him out of the car. When he comes over, I'll distract him so you can hop out and get to work on sneaking the eagle suit from his backseat. Then you bring it to the trunk of my car. You got that?"

"Yes, I think so," she said. "But won't he notice me stealing the suit?"

Exactly my sentiments, Cupid Delaney thought. This whole "plan" was about as unplanned as it could get. Yet poor innocent and trusting Helen had placed all her faith in Dawn.

As the light changed and the blue Camaro rolled down West Orange Avenue toward them, Cupid realized the trick. It was so simple, it was perfect. Pete Grayson would never get a chance to stop by their car and be duped by the Woodside girls because Pete Grayson was never going to stop. The blue Camaro had plenty of gas and would continue to roll, quite merrily, right past the red Mustang. It would roll past a falsely shocked and puzzled Dawn and go on its way to the West Orange stadium. Ted Abatto never emptied the gas tank. Dawn had not asked him to. If it came out later, she would frown and sputter and make excuses that she had specifically asked Helen to take care of the matter. If Helen hadn't asked Ted, why, it was anyone's guess, then, whose fault it really was.

How diabolical, Cupid Delaney thought. And also how cruel. Not only to have the stunt backfire, but to place the blame on unsuspecting Helen, an ugly little duckling only now beginning to come out of her shell and feel like a swan. No, the butterfly vowed, twitching her wings. I won't let Dawn get away with it. I'll think of something, anything, a spell, but what? And hurry, hurry, the blue Camaro was about to swing past the parked Mustang—and a secretly amused Dawn.

Just as Helen began to exclaim that the Camaro wasn't running out of gas and what was the matter, Dawn suddenly jerked to life. She put the key into the ignition, started the car, and swung out into traffic. Cupid Delaney hovered by her ear, murmuring silently, willing her powers to work. The Camaro tried to veer away, but the Mustang clipped it just enough to cause the boy to pull over.

"My word, that was quick thinking." Helen looked at Dawn with unconcealed admiration. "I never thought he'd stop. Wow. What are you going to do now?"

Dawn stared down at her hands blankly. Then she blinked in surprise. "I don't know."

"Well, whatever it is, it'll be great! Oh, this is so exciting!"

Dawn was still in shock over her unplanned accident. How could she have been stupid enough to pull out at the very moment that Pete Grayson was driving past? The very boy she wanted to avoid was now leaping from his car and stalking angrily to hers, brows knit together and obviously cursing under his breath.

Get it together! she admonished herself. You can still salvage the plan if you do some quick thinking. She could prevent the eagle costume from changing hands. It would be easy. Pete Grayson looked mad enough to put it on and claw out the lining of her specialized seat covers, then do a tap dance with his talons on the car hood. He'd certainly notice if an overexcited Helen tampered with the Camaro.

Dawn wasn't the only one thinking along these lines. So was Cupid Delaney. It was fine that she had gotten Pete Grayson to stop, but now what? As well intentioned as Helen was, she was new to the fine art of high school pranks. As sure as anything, she'd bungle the attempt to remove the mascot outfit. And Dawn certainly wouldn't help. No, Cupid would have to do something else and fast. Pete Grayson stood outside the Mustang, hands jammed into his parka, and motioned for Dawn to get out. With his feet stamping on the ground to get warm and his breath coming out in plumed vapors, he resembled a fire-breathing dragon.

Helen's cheeks were flushed with excitement. "What are you going to do, Dawn?"

The girl ignored her, frantically trying to plan her next move. But nothing came. No bright idea. No surefire plan of action. For once, in a crisis situation, her smarts had deserted her. Unbeknownst to her, a tiny butterfly hovered close to her ear and successfully scrambled her brain waves. But Cupid Delaney knew she had to do more. Scrambled brain waves weren't enough.

113

And then Helen craned her head out the window and murmured, "Gosh, he's kinda cute," giving Cupid Delaney her idea.

Dawn snapped, "Don't be ridiculous! He's nothing of the kind. He's . . ." She peered up into the boy's face. "Beautiful." Her voice trailed off. Her mouth fell open; her cheeks flushed. One hand hurriedly flew up to her hair and patted it in place. Her skin was tingling; her heart was aquiver. She had all the right symptoms: She was in love! Cupid Delaney giggled to herself. She hadn't lost her touch completely.

And the dark-haired, lean-featured boy with a scowl on his face obviously felt the same way. There was a smitten quality to his movements as the frown vanished and he opened Dawn's door and helped the girl out as if she were priceless Meissen china. They stood close together, shyly stealing looks at each other, beaming idiotically through a rainbow-colored haze.

"Uh, about the car," Dawn began, biting her lip in mute apology. But Pete shrugged, too mesmerized by Dawn's beauty to remember what caused him to pull over in the first place.

"What about it?" he said softly, his eyes never leaving her face. "It looks just fine to me."

"Me, too," Dawn said dreamily. Neither one made a move to check out the damages.

Helen, meanwhile, was not asleep at the switch. Thinking Dawn's accident and subsequent behavior were part of the revised plan, she edged out of the front seat and quickly walked over to the Camaro. Stealing peeks over her shoulder continually, she very slowly, very carefully opened the back door of the blue car. The hinge gave a loud creak. She froze, waiting for Pete's angry voice to bellow "Get out of there!" But he was too busy scribbling down Dawn's address and phone number. The couple looked more romantically entwined than the bride and groom dolls on a wedding cake.

"Gosh, she's something!" Helen giggled softly. "I think we're really going to pull it off!"

She turned back and carefully slid the eagle costume over her shoulder. It was a large, brownish gray suit with sewn-in cloth wings, and the separate head, complete with majestic glass eyes and lifelike beak, was heavy, but she could carry it. She glanced repeatedly at Dawn and Pete, but they were totally wrapped up in each other, oblivious to the outside world and to the prank being pulled off right in front of their noses. Well, Pete's nose. Dawn knew exactly what was happening. That was why she now had turned Pete to face in the opposite direction.

Helen gave a nervous cough and half walked, half skipped to the Mustang. The trunk wasn't open, as per the original plan, but she yanked open the front door and hurled the eagle outfit into the back.

"That takes care of you, Baldy," she said, dusting off her hands. But what about Dawn? The cheerleader was lost in conversation with Pete. Helen gnawed at her lower lip. What should she do? Tap Dawn on the shoulder and tell her they had to get going? But Pete would see the suit was gone in a flash and follow them. Should she let the lovebirds chatter on and drive off on her own? But Pete would eventually come back to earth and realize what had happened, and he still had the car. And Dawn had to cheer at the big game. Wouldn't she blow a fuse if she missed that?

Helen wavered, so Cupid Delaney stepped in. In no time flat Helen was starting Dawn's car and pulling away into traffic, leaving behind the movie version of *Romeo and Juliet Go 20,000 Leagues Under the Sea*. Helen felt a guilty pang but quickly squelched it. She had been assigned a mission impossible and she had done it! She had stolen the West Orange High School eagle and henceforth was a bona fide member of the Spirit Club. All the kids at school would be shocked but proud of her, and tomorrow night the boy of her dreams would escort her to the most important dance of the year, and everyone would see that she had made it. She, formerly the invisible Helen Mapes, was now Craig Lacrosse's girl and a vital entity all her own. Helen threw back her head and laughed aloud. She was so happy, so high in the sky, that she felt like doing something wild, something really fun and crazy and totally out of character. She glanced in the rearview mirror to make a turn and the eagle's glassy eyeballs stared into hers. That's it! she crowed. The eagle! No one, but no one, will believe what I'm going to do next.

Except for Cupid Delaney, whose powers were so drained she couldn't do anything but lie on the floor of the car in an exhausted heap of feelers and wings and pray that nothing too damaging to her mission would happen.

The big game had started ten minutes late, but the seat reserved for Helen was still empty. Alvin adjusted his muffler and peered gloomily around the stadium. What had happened to delay her? It wasn't like Helen to be late. She was always so punctual, one of the things Alvin cherished about her. That made her seem so much more mature than all the other silly, giggling, impulsive girls he knew. And now, here it was nearly 4:15, and no Helen in sight. And for that matter, no Dawn in sight either. He had noticed during the opening cheers that the usually prominent cheerleader was not among those present. What's going on? Alvin wondered.

West Orange fumbled a pass and the kids in the bleachers erupted into roars, but he hardly noticed. His mind was on the strange combination of Dawn and Helen, two instinctive opposites if he had ever seen them. Yet lately Helen had been raving about the girl. And Dawn had invited her to join the Spirit Club. Could the two be up to no good with this insane stunt they had discussed yesterday?

No, that was a wash. Both mascots were on the field cheering their respective teams. Granted, the West Orange eagle had shown up late, but he was there all right, strutting around, preening, making a fool of himself. By comparison, Woodside's pirate seemed tame. Mel Hendricks, with his hat, earring, and phony sword, just wasn't commanding the same attention that the eagle was. Yet now that Alvin really noticed, it was a weird kind of attention. Kids on both sides of the field were pointing and staring and laughing.

West Orange had just fumbled the ball, but the eagle was squawking like an enraged hen, holding its nose, or beak, as if smelling rotten eggs. The crazy bird was acting like its own team goofed intentionally. After the next play, the eagle behaved even more strangely. The Pirates' winning combination of Craig Lacrosse as quarterback and Sal Jimena as receiver brought off a first touchdown for Woodside. The kids exploded, jumping up and down and screaming, but the West Orange eagle drooped along the opponents' sideline, waving a white flag of surrender in its beak. That was crazy and morale-busting, especially coming from West Orange, and Alvin was not the only one to notice. Row upon row of Woodside kids cheered at this symbolic acknowledgment of defeat so early in the game, while the West Orange bleachers glowered and buzzed in a decidedly displeased manner. That didn't stop the eagle. When Woodside kicked the additional point over the goalpost, the great big bird flopped down on the ground and twitched in abject misery.

At this point, no one was watching the action *on* the field, but off. All eyes were focused on the eagle. The Woodside kids loved its antics; the West Orange kids hated them. And with good reason, Alvin agreed. He wouldn't want the pirate behaving so abominably and with a lack of faith and trust in his own team. It made West Orange look silly and undignified, and that was creating a negative impact on its players. They were repeatedly losing their concentration to watch the eagle shuffle, squawk, or droop by. Woodside was baffled, but happily so. The bird's antics made the Pirates pull together in a tight unit. Moments later two astonishing things happened at the same time: A bemused Alvin turned to find a bedraggled Cupid Delaney sitting beside him and Woodside scored its second touchdown.

Alvin was just exclaiming, "Wait a minute! What's going on?" when the eagle got jumped by two of the West Orange bench warmers for making *V* for victory signs with its wings and dancing a jig.

"What the heck's wrong with that mascot?" Alvin demanded. He glanced suspiciously at Cupid Delaney. "I bet you had something to do with it. Am I wrong?"

She drew herself up haughtily. "I have nothing whatsoever to do with the bird's behavior. That was entirely her own decision."

Alvin did a double take. "*Her?* You mean the West Orange mascot is a girl?"

"It is today."

"Then those guys shouldn't be chasing her. Look! They caught her and just tossed her over their shoulders!"

Bedlam reigned in the sidelines as the two irate West Orange players turned an angrily squawking eagle upside down. As the West Orange bleachers cheered, the head of the costume became detached and rolled off, exposing a very frightened and red-faced Helen to the crowd. Instant pandemonium. As the West Orange captors stared down at her in baffled horror, she wriggled out of their grip and began sprinting around the stadium.

"Who is it?" "I don't know. Grab her!" The pursuit was on.

Alvin jumped up, his face frozen. "Helen," he whispered. "No, it can't be. Not Helen!" He whirled on Cupid Delaney. "Tell me it isn't who I think it is."

She winced. She never seen Alvin so beside himself. Or so furious with her. Shamefaced, she nodded yes.

Alvin growled and sprang into action, Clark Kent about to leap to Lois Lane's defense.

"Helen!" he shouted. "I'm coming! Hang on!" Pushing aside bewildered, laughing kids, he jumped off the stands and made for the sidelines. But the West Orange lynch mob of two had swelled its ranks. Now about ten kids and cheerleaders joined forces and were chasing Helen. And Helen, clad in the cumbersome eagle suit, was losing ground. Within moments the West Orange group would catch her.

Alvin turned back to the stands and cupped his hands to his mouth.

"Cupid, please do something! Anything!" He made a helpless gesture, then raced to meet Helen, who was fast approaching the goalposts.

At the same time, the ball was in motion when Craig looked up and saw his beloved being pursued.

"Helen," he mouthed, standing still. All thoughts of the game evaporated. Ignoring the play, he dashed toward the goalposts, his arms outstretched, his eyes on Helen. Cupid Delaney twitched nervously in the stands. This was sure disaster if she had ever seen it. Helen was tiring and soon to be overcome by the West Orange kids; Alvin and Craig were both madly running toward the same point, calling out Helen's name.

Hurry! Hurry! Think! Cupid Delaney urged herself. You've got to save Helen. She scrunched up her face, shut her eyes very tight, and murmured some words. The stands shook and some people next to her said, "Earthquake?", but she ignored them. Her eyes were fixed on the official stadium clock. *Pffft. Pffft. Pffft.* The seconds flew by, blurred into minutes, and the halftime whistle sounded. As if on cue, fireworks exploded above the stadium to cries of delight, and the bandleaders of both school marching bands jerked awake and ordered their people to move, move, MOVE! and fall into formation on the field. There was a massive confluence of bodies and instruments, blaring into noise, almost drowning out the whine and popping of the fireworks display. The West Orange contingent was abruptly thwarted from achieving its goal. Helen darted to safety toward the Woodside goalposts just as Craig and Alvin both reached her.

"Honey Bunny!" the quarterback cried and opened his arms.

Honey Bunny? Shocked, Alvin turned his head, and in that split second, banged straight into the goalpost. The field tilted; stars flew in front of his face. He wobbled unsteadily and held out a hand.

"Helen?"

But Helen was securely wrapped inside Craig's arms, basking in his warm praise for pulling off the stunt.

"Helen?"

But Helen was responding to something Craig had just whispered. She threw her eagle wings around him and cried, "Oh I'd love to be your girl!"

Alvin felt the world slipping away, literally as well as figuratively. He took a baby step toward the embracing couple, them crumpled to the ground. Helen and Craig were totally oblivious. Gazing up, still seeing stars, he saw the distressed face of Cupid Delaney floating above him.

"Alvin! Are you all right? Can you talk to me?"

He reached up a rubbery hand and touched one of her cherub curls. "Ah, the girl of my dreams. Will you go to the Grid with me?" He blinked fuzzily, grinned a crooked grin, and then conked out.

Cupid Tells Alvin to
Take a Leap

"Hey, Helen, you're a heroine! Check out the front page of the *Bulletin*!" Tom Delacruz held the school paper close to Helen's puzzled face. She and Craig were holding hands, ambling through the main wing after second period. Now the flustered girl put her hands to her cheeks when she saw the three-quarter-page photograph of herself in eagle costume, defiantly making victory signs over a Woodside touchdown. The caption read: Even Big Bird Knows a Winner When He Sees One.

Helen nervously blinked. "This doesn't mention my name, does it?"

Tom laughed. "Relax. The article describes your behavior yesterday in all too glowing terms, but it doesn't give any Spirit Club secrets away. Oh, sure, most of the kids know. That's all they've been talking about this morning, that and the dance tonight, but no one wants to get you in trouble with the administration, so we're all playing dumb. Hey, enjoy the glory. You deserve it."

"She sure does." Craig placed an arm around her shoulders. "I still can't believe you pulled it off."

Helen lifted her hand in modest dismissal. "I keep telling you I didn't do it. Dawn is the one who deserves all the credit. She pulled it off, not me. You should have seen her stop Pete Grayson yesterday. She dented her car and pretended to fall in love with the poor guy, all for the sake of the stunt. She even missed the game! Just to keep Pete occupied. She's really wonderful."

"Yeah, well, you're the one who thought of wearing the eagle suit at the game. No one told you to do that. And you're the one who disrupted West Orange's game. You were hilarious during the first quarter." Tom shrugged and grinned. "I only wish I hadn't been playing so much so I could have caught your complete act. I hear *People* magazine is making noises about a story on you."

They all laughed, Helen giggling in the Goldilocks fashion that would have once grated on Dawn's nerves. But the cheerleader only smiled at the sound as she approached the group. *Smiled* would be too weak a word, Cupid Delaney decided, perched inside Helen's large tote bag. No, Dawn didn't smile. She glowed. She radiated loving feelings for everyone in her path, including Helen Mapes.

The others might be confused by the Miss Congeniality role, but Cupid Delaney knew the reason why. After all, she had played matchmaker between Pete and Dawn. The spell had worked perfectly, so perfectly that she hesitated to revoke it. Dawn seriously believed that she and the West Orange boy had a mutual attraction for each other. Hadn't she impulsively asked him to the Grid and hadn't he just as impulsively accepted? She had failed to get to the big game; her mind (and heart) were occupied elsewhere. If she felt guilty at all, she only had to imagine Pete's handsome face before her and then the niggling feelings went away. If Cupid Delaney were to lift the spell, Dawn would plummet to earth with depressing rapidity. Her romantic encounter with Pete would be revealed as a joke, and she would question her sanity in getting involved so quickly with a member of the enemy camp. Without the validity of her feelings for the boy, her cheerleading friends might reconsider her negligent actions under a far grimmer light and bounce her from the squad; Spirit Club might demote her and, far, far worse, she would have no date for the Grid.

To make matters even more difficult, mousy creature Helen not only had Craig in the palm of her hand, but also the whole school. Her daring originality with the eagle costume had scored a hit among the kids. The school paper had splashed the incident all over the front page, and there was talk the decorating committee would add an eagle motif to the usual homecoming themes. Giggling Goldilocks would float into the Grid on the arm of Craig a reigning princess and would float out again at the end of the evening on the arm of the homecoming king. And Dawn, if she even chose to brave the dance at all, would make the loneliest, glummest homecoming queen. No, the tiny butterfly decided, I must take pity on the girl. As selfish and as cruel as she seemed, she was really insecure about her image. And she had learned her lesson by seeing Helen shine so brightly in the Woodside galaxy. Dawn would go to the dance with her date and have a perfectly wonderful time. Afterwards, when the spell wore off (as all spells do, having a thirty-day expiration date), she could pick up the pieces and start anew. As I'll be doing myself, Cupid Delaney realized. In thirty days—less!—I'll be a fully certified cupid with permanent angelic wings and the authority to pick my own missions.

Somehow, instead of feeling lighthearted about her future, she felt seized by doubts. Did she really have the makings of a true Love Bureau emissary? The submissiveness to respond to Sweetheart Squad leaders' orders? The singlemindedness to banish all her feelings for Alvin? She gave a mental shake of her head. She had to. That was all there was to it. A cupid trainee was what she was, and a certified cupid was what she was going to be. And no more questioning. Valentina wouldn't like her decision to match Dawn with Pete Grayson, but there were extenuating circumstances. And it was a positive given that Craig Lacrosse, the school heartbreaker, had fallen head over heels in love with Helen Mapes and was escorting her to the Grid. The mission was only fifty percent complete, but Cupid Delaney prayed that percent was strong enough to persuade Valentina to pass her.

Now she sat up straighter inside the unzipped portion of the bag and gazed with alert eyes at Dawn, who was joining the group.

Craig tightened his hold around Helen's shoulders, as if to say: Don't make another scene. You know this is my girl.

But Dawn surprised everyone, including herself, by going up to Helen and giving her a light peck. "I heard you were fantastic!" She smiled warmly at the dazed girl. "You were a hit. Congratulations! I wouldn't have thought to take the stunt one step further."

Tension in the air noticeably lessened. Helen beamed back and giggled. "Did your friend get in trouble?"

"Eagle Man Pete?" Dawn all but licked her lips. "He's coping. One tough guy. Just as I knew he was.

125

You'll be seeing him tonight at the dance. Why not ask him then?"

Helen blushed. "Oh, no, I couldn't. No, I'd be too embarrassed. I mean, I *stole* his costume."

"The school's costume, not his. And I'm telling you, he understands. He even thinks it's funny. And he admires you. I guess we all do. Well, I've got D'Andrea next, so I've got to go." She hesitated, looked over at Craig, and took a deep breath. "I never thought I'd be saying this to you, but have a good time tonight. I really mean it. Both of you. And Craig, I hope you're voted homecoming king."

The quarterback was visibly surprised. He cleared his throat. "Thank you, Dawn. And good luck to you, too. We might still have the first official dance together as Woodside royalty. That is, if your date won't mind . . . ?"

A firm nod of the head, a happy laugh, and she was gone. Tom and Craig exchanged puzzled smiles.

"Man, I never thought," Craig murmured, looking after her. "I mean, after the scene yesterday outside the cafeteria. Wow."

"I *told* you she was wonderful," Helen chirped. "And I can't wait to see her with Pete tonight. It really should be something."

"It'll be something, all right." Tom lifted a shoulder and looked at Craig. "Yeah, I get the feeling this Grid will be one we won't forget for a long time."

"You can say that again," Cupid Delaney mumbled under her breath. She carefully inched her way out of Helen's bag, stood poised on the edge to get her bearings, then took off for the boys' gym.

Alvin yanked up his drooping shorts and eyed the parallel bars with distaste. He glanced around

126

the gym and muttered. Pommel horses, rings, and the beam all seemed to stare back at him with disdain. Go on, they sneered, I dare you. Third period P.E. was his worst hour of the day, and he especially dreaded Coach Winship's gymnastics class. But what could he do? No one wanted to recognize chess as a viable athletic substitute, so he was stuck, four times a week, with a bunch of goons who loved to leap, twist, and throw their bodies into very torturous positions.

There was a frosh basketball game going on in one part of the cavernous gym, and in another, a volleyball tournament. Edging out of Coach Winship's line of vision, he began to move toward the volleyball area when he felt a tap on his shoulder. He whirled around to confront Cupid Delaney.

"I told you never to do that!" Alvin gasped, clutching at his heart. "And what are you popping up here for, in the flesh, no less? You want me to get expelled or something?"

She gave a tinkling laugh.

"Hey, Danziger!" yelled Coach Winship. "Quit yapping to yourself and get going on the vault. Today you're really going to do it, not just talk about it."

Alvin moaned and thrust a hand through his unruly hair. "Two 'Ripley's Believe It or Not' events in one morning: I get to talk to the Invisible Woman and probably damage myself for life by taking on the dreaded vault. Not to mention my near concussion yesterday and watching Helen run off with Craig in an eagle suit. I can't take too much more of this, you know that?"

"You won't have to," Cupid Delaney said in a soft, unhappy voice. "I'm leaving tonight."

Alvin stopped dead. Then he motioned her to a more private part of the gym. "But you'll be coming back, won't you?" he said, as lightly as he could. "And probably bringing some Ecstasy Embassy reinforcements with you?"

Cupid Delaney lifted her head and looked at Alvin. "I know when I'm beaten where a strong-willed subject is concerned. And you're quite possibly the most stubborn, strong-willed subject I've ever met. If my powers can't make you fall for Dawn, then I'm not needed any longer. It's as simple as that. Besides, I feel bad enough about your accident yesterday. I should have prevented it."

Alvin rubbed the tiny bump on his forehead and grinned. "This little number isn't your fault. You did everything you could to save Helen's skin and I appreciate it. All those fireworks and then the bands crashing onto the field. It was unbelievable. But Lover Boy Lacrosse running up to Helen and moaning 'Honey Bunny' was too much. I looked back at Helen to see if she thought it was as ridiculous as I did, and—bam!—that's when I got it!"

"Does it still hurt?"

"Not as much as this insane situation with Craig and Helen. Anyway," he said stiffly, "what do you care? You won't be around to play Florence Nightingale."

There was a long pause, during which time Cupid Delaney wanted to say, "But I want to be." How could she stand here and reveal her true feelings to this boy when she knew her mission was almost over? No, it was impossible, ill-fated, and in the worst possible Love Bureau taste. But Alvin was so adorable, and she could swear there was *something* flickering in those warm eyes of his, a private message for her?

"I care, Alvin," she said softly.

128

His eyes lit up. Hope springs eternal, but it was dashed immediately at the red-haired boy's next words.

"Good, because if you do—really care, I mean—then you'll do something about Helen and me. Please, Cupid, you helped her before; now help both of us. It's not right that this athletic jerk should string Helen along, play her boyfriend, when he doesn't even know the girl! He doesn't even look at Helen and see her. All he sees is what you've told him to see, but that's not reality. That's fantasy; that's magic. Don't you think Helen is going to be crushed when Craig wakes up and dumps her sometime down the road? Because sure as his ego is as big as the Empire State Building, he's going to revert back to type and pull his usual girl-hopping number. And Helen will be left in the dust, a victim." Alvin's voice rose. "I ask you, is that fair or right? Is your Love Bureau so callous as to barge in and twist people's lives around, regardless of the consequences? Who are you to play love roulette with our hearts?"

Cupid Delaney was taken aback. She had never received this kind of criticism before, especially not directed toward one of the most sacred, inviolable institutions in the heavens. All her other subjects had blessed the Bureau's skillful matchmaking. Thank-you notes constantly spilled into the special mail branch, postmarked from every spot on the continent. There were wedding invitations piled up in huge batches on the squad leaders' desks. Not one subject had ever thought to complain or point out the harsher side of the Love Bureau's methods because no single subject had ever been unhappily paired before. Or so the official line of the Love Bureau went. Maybe poorly matched couples were just too scared to step forward and admit it. Cupid Delaney bit her lip and frowned.

Alvin saw her weaken and pressed on. "Anyway, did you ever check the credentials of these love dictators? Are they human beings? Can they fall in love, marry, and have children? Can they ever really know deep down what it's like to want a person who's confused and doesn't realize the attraction herself? And instead of trying to understand and helping the two of you get together, they send a mythical creature to interrupt your life and suddenly begin changing all your channels. I tell you, it's unfair and cruel. I know Helen and Craig are not suited at all and you know it too. I can tell that you do."

There was a tiny hesitation, and then Cupid Delaney said carefully, "That may be true—"

"Aha!"

"—but can you honestly say that you and Helen are any better suited? I know, I know"—she held up a restraining hand when he started to speak—"you're going to tell me about the mutual interests and the same hobbies, but, Alvin, please stop and think. Did Helen sincerely want to study every Saturday night at the library? Did she really want to go to the train exhibit with you? And if she had gone, would she have had as much fun as you and I did?"

For a moment, a twinkle gleamed in Alvin's eye at the memory of the infamous train ride. But then his face darkened.

Cupid Delaney hurriedly continued. "And if Helen is the gentle, quiet, stay-at-home person you swear she is, why did she jump at the chance to join Spirit Club? Or go out and buy completely new clothes and makeup and become friendly with Dawn and Wendy and Claire? What possessed her to put on the eagle costume and clown around at the big game? Is that the shy, steady girl you know?"

Alvin swallowed. "Well, no, but, but—that's your influence!"

Cupid Delaney shook her head. "I had nothing to do with Helen's personality, Alvin. I didn't force her to attend the Spirit Club meeting or to agree to steal the West Orange mascot." She hesitated. "And I didn't force her to go out with Craig or be his date for the Grid tonight."

Alvin's mouth tightened. "No, but she would never have had these crazy mood changes if you hadn't shazaamed Craig or whatever it was you did and he hadn't come on to her. She would have gone on like before, sweet and natural, not like the phonies she's hanging around with. And I want you, no, I *need* you to do something. Please, you've got to."

"Danziger!" roared Coach Winship. A pair of ice blue eyes impaled him from across the room. "Get to the vault. Now."

Alvin rolled his eyes but began to shuffle as slowly as possible to the much-dreaded object of torture. Cupid Delaney kept pace with him, a guard walking the prisoner to the place of execution. Her heart twisted within her at Alvin's depressed expression. She had to do something to help him, but what? As he neared the group of boys waiting in line for the vault, she leaned over and whispered, "What do you want me to do? If it's in my power, I'll help you."

She heard a warning rumble of thunder far away. Valentina acting up again, listening in and expressing her disapproval? Cupid Delaney squared her shoulders and ignored the long-distance message.

"Tell me," she urged him.

Alvin bent over in the pretense of tying a shoelace, allowing the other boys to get in front of him. Cupid bent over, too, their heads inches apart. For a moment, their eyes locked and something warm and alive danced in the air between them. I knew it! Cupid Delaney exulted inwardly. He cares! He cares about me! He wants to kiss me!

But Alvin quickly shook himself, breaking the spell. A shutter closed down behind the glasses.

"I only want one thing," he said fiercely. "I want you to change Craig back into the boor he was on Monday. Before you put the spell on him at the football practice."

"Oh, but I can't. *I can't.*"

"Yes, you can. You can do anything, remember?"

Cupid Delaney frowned as she straightened up. She rubbed one white boot nervously against the other.

"Come *on,* Cupid," Alvin persisted. He was slowly but surely being jostled to the front of the line where the dreaded vault and an impatient Coach Winship waited.

"Give us all a chance, can't you? Let us decide our own fates. Remove the spell from Craig. Let Helen know the kind of person he really is. Let her make up her own mind about the dance. If you believe in true love, you'll do it."

"True love is my motto," Cupid Delaney said uneasily. "But . . ."

"But nothing," Alvin retorted. "Then you'll let true love, not magic, manufactured love, run its course. Please?" One last imploring look before Coach Winship called, "All right, Danziger, you're next."

Cupid Delaney watched as Alvin tensed and then did some quick knee bends. There was something so vulnerable in his movements that her heart seemed to melt within her.

I'm crazy about this boy, and he's in love with another girl, she thought. Yet I like him so much, I want him to be happy, regardless of what happens to me. Does being willing to possibly fail my mission mean I'm seriously falling in love?

The rumbling thunder cracked overhead.

"Go ahead, laugh, Valentina Amour," Cupid Delaney whispered. "I'm sure you think I'm crazy where my romantic responsibilities are concerned. But I know the consequences if I revoke the spell on Craig, and Helen returns to Alvin. It's my mission and my decision to make."

The sounds of the storm deepened, then faded away.

Cupid Delaney nodded and squared her chin. Whew! The wrath of the Sweetheart Squad leader was something to behold. Cupid Delaney was lucky she was down here on earth and not within oath-carrying range of the majestic semigoddess. But Valentina might not have to lose her overwhelming temper yet. There was too much at stake to make such an important decision within seconds.

Just before Alvin pushed off, she ran up to him and whispered, "I'll think about it."

"But—"

"But nothing. Just thinking about it is a major step for me. Now let's do your vault. And let's do it perfectly."

Before Alvin had a chance to speak or pull back, Cupid Delaney put her hand in his trembling one. Like Peter Pan teaching Wendy to fly, she had him racing surefootedly to the vault and, without a second's pause, miraculously lifting over in one graceful, flawless swoop. There was stunned silence among the gymnastics students. Coach Winship stood off to one side, the whistle dangling from his rounded lips.

Alvin straightened up and grinned at Cupid Delaney. He squeezed her hand before releasing it.

"Hey, Cupid, you never fail to amaze me," he said softly, turning aside. "Now if you can pull off this other stunt with Craig as easily as you did this, I'll adore you forever."

She winced but managed a smile. "Just remember one thing: If it doesn't work out tonight the way you want it to, it's really not my vault."

As Alvin groaned, she—snap!—transformed herself into a butterfly and fluttered quickly away.

True Romance at
the High School Dance

For the first time in her life, Cupid Delaney was
jealous of one of her subjects. It was insane, it was
unheard of in Love Bureau circles, but it was true
and happening to her right at this very moment:
eight o'clock on the night of the Woodside Grid.
With more green in her wings than her usual yellow,
black, and orange, the little butterfly watched as
Helen put the finishing touches to her outfit.

The formerly colorless girl had really outdone
herself tonight. Not only had she had her 1970s
hairdo cut and professionally styled, but she had
spent hours with her makeup, poring intently over
cosmetic ads in fashion magazines and dragging in
Dorothy and Ethel to witness each new daring
application of color. When her face was done—a
surprising transformation, Cupid Delaney had to
admit—Helen slipped into the new dress Dawn had
helped her select after school. It was outrageously
expensive but well worth her depleted funds. Dawn
had excellent, if somewhat theatrical taste, and had
chosen a slinky silk kimono for Helen, a brilliant
crimson, black, and white number that seemed to
accentuate all the right curves and skillfully hide all

the wrong ones. With her new lace-up black sandals and bright red bangle earrings, the metamorphosis of nerdette to gorgeous girl was complete. Helen looked like she belonged in Craig's league now— well, if not the Major, then perhaps the Little. But would she want to stay there once lovey-dovey Dr. Jekyll turned into girl-hungry Mr. Hyde? And the even bigger question: Once his spell was removed, would Lover Boy Lacrosse take one look at Helen and start doubting his sanity in having her as his date for the dance? Would he make a scene and send Helen hurtling back to the security of Alvin's arms?

What if . . . ? Cupid Delaney considered all of the possible outcomes to her actions but could not begin to guess which way the wind would blow for tonight. She had thought at the outset of the week that she had gotten a pretty good handle on her four subjects and could successfully gauge their reactions, but now she realized that she had made a very grave mistake: Like all Love Bureau representatives, she had stereotyped and categorized these human beings. She had left no room for free will or deliberate choice on their part. Granted, Helen had secretly yearned to be Craig's girl, so her behavior was more predictable. But Alvin and Dawn? That was quite another story. Both the nerd and hunkette had made her rethink the purpose behind her mission. As Alvin had remarked, was it right that the Love Bureau should interfere so blithely with mortal lives without giving them any say in the matter? Who knew better about finding happiness: detached heavenly bodies with no one to hug or human beings who made commitments and took the risk of getting hurt?

One look at Helen answered the question. She was all aquiver with the excitement and anticipation of her first big date. She was humming gaily under her breath, her big gray eyes luminous and spar-kling. Cupid Delaney didn't blame her. If she were in her shoes, she'd be floating, too. Only she would be dreaming about Alvin picking her up. Alvin coming to the door, looking adorable and touch-ingly stiff in a rented tux. Alvin catching his first glimpse of her dressed up in something other than the all-white regulation cupid attire. She had always been pleased with the uniform, cleaning bills aside, but another color, another style, might be more flattering to her pastel tones. Oh, she envied Helen's radiance tonight. She'd give anything to turn in her shimmery tunic and her magic power for the all-too-mortal joy of dancing close to a special boy.

That will never be, she admonished herself. So quit dragging your wings around Helen's bedroom and brighten up. If all goes well tonight, you'll own the golden wings of a cupid. And Woodside and dances and Alvin Danziger will soon fade away.

A phone rang in the Mapeses' house and Helen half rose.

Mrs. Mapes called, "Helen, for you!"

She leapt up. "Is it Craig?"

Her mother poked her head in the bedroom door. "No the other one. Alvin. The one who talks out loud to himself."

"Oh, Alvin." Her shoulders drooped. She walked slowly to the door. "I wonder what he wants?"

Mrs. Mapes frowned. "I don't know, but he sure sounds funny. He asked me how you were."

Helen reached the kitchen and, giving her mother a puzzled shrug, picked up the receiver and said hello.

"Helen, are you all right? Is everything OK?" Alvin burst out.

Her eyebrows rose. "Why shouldn't it be?"

The small butterfly that rode in the pocket of Mrs. Mapes' apron extended her auditory sensors to pick up Alvin's end of the conversation. It wasn't difficult. He was babbling so loudly Mrs. Mapes could hear him. And Ethel, standing near the refrigerator, rolled her eyes as she bit into an apple.

"Well, I don't know," he sputtered. "I mean, didn't anything happen this afternoon to Craig?"

"What would happen?" She gave an exasperated sigh. "Honestly, Alvin, are you still going on about the invisible creatures who have hypnotized Craig? Because I don't have time for it. It's after eight and I'm getting ready to leave."

"You're still going to the dance and Craig is taking you?"

"Well, of course I am. Unless something's happened that I don't know about? Has something happened to Craig, something you're not telling me?" Her voice rose to such a frightened squeak that Alvin hastened to reassure her.

"Oh, no, nothing. Nothing. I'm sorry, Helen. I thought— Oh, forget what I thought."

Cupid heard Helen mumble something and then hang up.

"Well, I don't understand the boy," Chloris Mapes clucked. "Calling you and making you all nervous before your big dance. I don't understand him at all."

Helen shook her head. "I don't either. Especially the one thing he asked before he hung up."

"What, Helen? What did he say?" Ethel asked.

"Maybe I misunderstood, but he said something about a butterfly. Something like have we seen a butterfly in the house tonight."

Ethel giggled as Mrs. Mapes waggled her eyebrows.

"Butterflies? In late November? That boy is getting stranger by the minute. Butterflies, indeed!"

Cupid Delaney held her breath and thought rapidly. She didn't like the sound of that conversation at all. Poor Alvin had probably assumed she had left his P.E. class that morning to locate Craig and remove the spell. By his way of thinking, Craig would have woken up to the reality of taking a V.U.P. (Very Unimportant Person) to the Grid and promptly called the date off, thereby squelching Helen's dreams. But that, alas, had not happened. Cupid Delaney had been tormented by indecision but had not taken action. All her life she had trained to be a certified cupid. And now tonight she had to make a decision that might alter all her dreams. What to do? What to do? She paced nervously inside the capacious apron pocket.

One thing she had to do, regardless of whatever else she decided this evening, was to get to the dance before any fireworks happened. Knowing Alvin so well now, she feared the boy might take matters into his own hands and confront Craig. And if that happened, well—she didn't want to consider the outcome. The doorbell rang, interrupting her thoughts.

"Craig!" Helen cried. "Oh, Mommy, he's here!"

Mrs. Mapes patted her on the shoulder. "You look lovely. I'll just go and let him in."

The Great Escape, Cupid Delaney realized. What perfect timing. Taking a deep breath, she cautiously inched her way out of Mrs. Mapes' apron and then, as Craig greeted Mrs. Mapes on the doorstep, swooped out into the cold, clear November night.

* * *

The Woodside gym had undergone major cosmetic surgery and now resembled the Athenian forest in Shakespeare's *Midsummer Night's Dream*. The bleacher sections had been lavishly garlanded with leafy green crepe paper and half-hidden by rented plants, some of which sat in tubs and resembled small trees. There were larger cardboard trees placed strategically near trailing ivy, and strings of lights overhead twinkled like stars. Lanterns hung from wooden posts, lending a garden air to the atmosphere, and someone had cleverly painted signs that read: PUCK'S PLACE and NO TRESPASSING AT TITANIA'S. It was all very festive and rather amateurish and Cupid Delaney felt a lump in her throat. Really, it was absurd to be so touched by such sophomoric window dressing but she was.

Darting around the gym, she magically altered the wattage of the lanterns until the room glowed as if by moonlight. Then she concentrated on the plant life and within seconds had lusher and healthier specimens. All in all, it looked like a perfect setting for the most important dance of the year. Sensing a quivering in her romantic pulsars, she turned and saw Tom Delacruz and his date, a pretty blonde, come in. Right on their heels were Dawn and Pete Grayson, followed by Wendy Chu and Ted Abatto. One subject here, Cupid Delaney thought, three to go.

The tiny butterfly flew quickly to the scene of the action.

"Hey, everybody," Dawn was saying, "a special person for you to meet. Well, he's special to *me*. Peter Grayson."

If her group knew all too well who the boy was and what he did for the rival school, they gave no indication. There were friendly introductions all around.

A stream of students poured in, and then there they were: the Odd Couple of Woodside High. Everyone stopped and stared. Craig's perfectly groomed golden brown hair gleamed above the crowd, a flag signaling his arrival. On his arm was a happily oblivious Helen, resplendent in her slinky kimono.

"Helen!" Dawn cried with geniune warmth in her voice. She waved and pointed to Peter. "Over here. A person you have a lot in common with!"

Helen groaned and hesitated but, clutching Craig's hand for support, went over. Dawn gave her a hug.

"Wow, you look fabulous! Doesn't she look pretty, Pete?"

The West Orange boy appraised the tense girl solemnly. "Different than the last time we, er, *bumped* into each other. And much different than the pictures in the paper Dawn showed me."

Helen blushed, but Pete laughed.

"She did such a great job that I've been thinking," Dawn said. "Spirit Club has a hard-working president, all modesty aside, but I could use a V.P. Someone to help with other crazy ideas and stunts. And, Helen, I think our whole group agrees you'd be perfect in that office."

"What?" She was taken aback, afraid it was a joke. But Craig squeezed her hand and Ted, Wendy, and Tom congratulated her. For a moment Helen's eyes looked suspiciously moist.

Cupid Delaney felt equally as moved but for a different reason. How far Dawn had come to suggest such a thing. The cheerleader's new attitude had much to do with caring about a boy and feeling more secure about herself. And if Cupid Delaney had had a hand in that, even inadvertently, she was very pleased.

Far up in the heavens, however, someone else was not so pleased. A slow-burning Valentina was staring in horror at the video screen.

"Who in Zeus' name is that pipsqueak with Dawn? The one practically glued to her arm?" Her voice rose. "That isn't Alvin! Alvin Danziger's supposed to be her date, not some gormless interloper!" She flung out a hand, and the cherubs peeling off the foil on her chocolate kisses exchanged frightened glances. At a signal from Valentina, they scattered. The Sweetheart Squad leader stood up and hurled her paperback romance to the ground.

"Enchantée! Passionata! Bella Rosa!" she bellowed. "Get in here, quick!"

In seconds the three senior Sweetheart leaders tumbled into the room. Valentina pointed a trembling finger at the video screen. "I can't believe my eyes or ears, but Delaney's doing it again! Making a disaster of her mission. Just watch with me. Oh, it's too ghastly . . . there!" She nodded at the screen as . . .

. . . an obviously distraught Alvin strode into the gym. He was wearing what looked like his father's college blazer, a shiny navy thing with an insignia on the wide lapels, rumpled corduroy pants, a wide maroon tie, and tennis shoes freshly spray-painted black. His reddish gold hair stuck up in points and his normally soft brown eyes glittered dangerously. Kids nudged each other as he came in, but he didn't notice. He was too busy scanning the gym for one person. When he found her, he nodded once to himself and wended his way through the crowd.

Cupid Delaney spotted Alvin at the same time he located Helen. Holding her breath, she soared over just as Alvin approached the couple. He stood off to one side, observing Helen and Craig, a woebegone look on his face. All the fury and fight had gone out of him. Instead, he resembled a kitten caught in a downpour—miserable, lonely, and all wet.

It was at that moment that Cupid Delaney decided to act. Was it fair that Alvin would never know Helen's true feelings for Craig? That he should go along assuming she was the only girl for him, when, in fact, there were so many other more compatible girls? And, more to the point, his comments about Love Bureau tactics touched a nerve. Perhaps there was more truth to what he said than she wanted to believe. Who gave Valentina Amour the right to rule the romantic roost with such an iron hand? She never listened to her subordinates on conflicting points of view; she never allowed the subjects to follow their own hearts. Well, this time they would, the tiny butterfly vowed. It may cost me my wings, but it'll be worth it to show Alvin I care.

Before she could act, however, Mr. Dalton, the rotund, perspiring principal, had stepped to the mike. He greeted everyone and then asked the eight candidates for homecoming court to approach the stage.

"Beautiful one, that's you." Pete proudly nudged Dawn.

Craig was leaning over, murmuring to Helen, when Cupid Delaney flew into view.

"Hey!" Ted exclaimed, looking up. "The decorating committee went all out this time. They rented exotic butterflies!"

Alvin's head spun around. Hope flared in his eyes. He elbowed his way through the crowd to get closer to Helen. "She's going to do it," he mumbled. "Cupid's really going to do it."

He sidled in next to Helen just as Craig was saying, "No matter if I win as king, you get my first dance."

Helen absorbed his words like a hungry flower soaking up sunshine.

Grinding his teeth, Alvin shouldered his way into the charmed circle.

"First dance goes to me and Helen makes up her own mind."

Craig's eyes narrowed. "What are you talking about, Danziger? Helen knows that I—"

His voice trailed off, his body froze, as Cupid Delaney flashed into action. Alvin stood by as all the members in the group stilled, like mannequins in a store window. The little butterfly hurriedly scrunched her features together and concentrated on the magic words . . .

. . . while above, Valentina rose from her chair. Her green eyes glittered in outrage. "How dare she even consider going against an order? Why, that little rebel! That—that baby-faced traitor! She thinks she's going to revoke Craig's spell. Well, think again, Cupid Benedict Arnold Delaney!" She flung her head back and chanted loudly. Thunder crashed. A wind howled, and . . .

. . . like a Keystone Kop movie, the action in the gym revved into fast forward as Craig blinked his eyes and gazed blankly at Helen. He frowned and, with a delicate shudder, removed her clinging arm like it was a tentacle of an octopus. Helen's brow puckered.

"Craig?" she whimpered. "Honey Bunny?"

Already the handsome senior was ogling Dawn's snug gown, ignoring Helen's plaintive

144

cries. Alvin observed the scene and rubbed his hands together.

"Be my date, Helen," he cried. "This guy's all wrong for you!"

But Helen shook her head, still gazing in adoration at Craig, who was now admiring the neckline of Wendy's dress.

"Craig!" Helen said, tugging at his sleeve. "Honey Bunny?"

The boy swiveled around to make a sarcastic retort, when his eyes widened and he took a step back.

"Helen?" he asked weakly, shaking his head as if to clear it. "What happened? I felt so funny for a few minutes. But now that you're here, everything's fine. Now, don't go away. After the voting's over, I'll come back and get you for our first dance, all right? And this creep"—he growled at Alvin—"can just buzz off."

As Helen nodded happily, Alvin slumped beside her.

"She failed," he muttered to himself. "Cupid tried but failed."

"I failed," Cupid Delaney echoed. She flew in dejected circles above Alvin's head. "Valentina found out and squelched my plan. I'm a goner now. A real loser. I've lost my dreams of flying up and of making Alvin happy. I've lost everything."

Stifling a sniffle, she heard her summons. It was time to go back and face Valentina's ire. Would she order Cupid Delaney out of the Love Bureau on the spot or grant her a lowly cherub's position, cleaning wings, peeling grapes and chocolate kisses, polishing white boots? Oh, it was too loathsome to contemplate. But the cruelest task was yet to come: bidding farewell to Alvin.

She fluttered sadly in front of his face. "Good-bye," she breathed into his ear.

"Hey," he whispered with alarm, "you're not leaving, are you? Can't you stay and dance just one dance with me?"

She hesitated, but Valentina's raspy command rang in her ear, "The mission is over. Report to me immediately."

Feeling brokenhearted, Cupid Delaney perched a moment on Alvin's glasses. "I'll miss you," she whispered. "I'll miss you." She fluttered her wings, once, twice in a light butterfly kiss on his cheek, then flew off through the open doors.

"Wait!" Alvin cried, dazedly touching his cheek. "Hey, Cupid, I'll miss you, too! Cupid . . ."

He ran to the exit but failed to locate the tiny dot of color. With a slump to his shoulders, he stood gazing up into the night.

While above . . .

. . . *"Oh, I hate unhappy endings," Passionata was sobbing. "It's just so sad." She reached for a tissue and blew her nose loudly.*

"Poor little Delaney," Enchantée blurted, her eyes filling with tears.

"Poor Alvin." Bella Rosa sighed, then wailed, "Oh, poor Alvin and Delaney!"

"Oh, poor me!" Valentina shouted. "Having to put up with all this hysteria and weeping. I haven't heard such mourning since Romeo and Juliet kicked the bucket. Now, pull yourselves together. Delaney deserves what she's going to get."

Bella Rosa raised a tearstained face. "But she's in love, Valentina! Surely she's been punished enough. She did what she did because of Alvin. She sacrificed everything. Doesn't that move you at all?"

"And Helen's so happy, and Craig appears to be, too," inserted Enchantée. *"And look at Dawn! Go on, look at her! She's floating on air."*

"Enough! Enough!" Valentina paced furiously, all the while stealing looks at the video screen and a desolate Alvin, still gazing up into the sky. She stopped, deliberated a minute, then flung herself down at a console.

"All right, get closer, all you sniveling romantics! So you can see what a really happy ending looks like!"

Giggling and clapping, the cupid leaders clustered around Valentina and stared at the screen . . .

. . . as Alvin felt a light tap on his shoulder.

He wheeled around to confront a vision: beautiful blonde Cupid Delaney dressed in a pale pink ruffled dress that bared one shoulder and looked both innocent and alluring.

"Wow," he breathed. "Well, if it isn't my dream girl. What's going on? Here to work more magic on Craig?"

Her heart sank. "Do you want me to?"

"No way." Alvin glanced into the gym and grinned. "I saw how Helen really feels about Craig. I guess I was never what she wanted at all. I hate to admit it, but she really wasn't the right girl for me."

"Oh," Cupid Delaney said softly, gazing anywhere but at Alvin.

"Maybe I shouldn't ask this, if it's a secret mission you're on or something," Alvin babbled, "but will you be around for a while, Cupid? Tonight, I mean?" His eyes looked so hopeful that she blushed.

"It's not Cupid any longer. It's Delaney. And yes, I'm going to be around for quite some time. The Love Bureau is letting me transfer to Woodside High for a year."

Alvin's face lit up. "That's fantastic! I can't believe it!" He shyly stretched out his hand and she took it. They both felt the tingle at the same time and laughed.

"So you're going to be in my classes maybe, eating lunch at the same time. Any plans for who you'd like to date?"

She nodded, staring straight into his eyes. He smiled and took hold of both her hands.

"Well, that sounds fine to me, but I have to ask you one very important thing before we make it official."

She looked at him, puzzled. "And that is . . . ?"

"Are you going to be my girl next term or are you going to go flitting around like a social butterfly?"

She laughed and as they lightly kissed, Delaney swore she heard a pleased sigh somewhere high overhead in the star-studded heavens.

ABOUT THE AUTHOR

"It was a disheartening day," says author Ellen Leroe. "True love had proved fickle, and I was feeling glum. Then I noticed a butterfly flying above me as I walked down the street. Cupid in disguise? I thought. What if—I played the writer's game—what if a real cupid were assigned to Earth to match two pairs of teenagers but had to perform her tasks under cover as a butterfly? Forgetting my gloomy thoughts, I began to write this book. And ever since I wrote it, that tiny butterfly has been following me!"

Ms. Leroe lives in San Francisco. Books she has written include *Confessions of a Teenage TV Addict*, *The Plot Against the Pom-Pom Queen*, and *Personal Business*, available in a Bantam Starfire edition.